THE CAREGIVER

Also by Shelley Shepard Gray

Sisters of the Heart series
HIDDEN
WANTED
FORGIVEN
GRACE

Seasons of Sugarcreek series
WINTER'S AWAKENING
SPRING'S RENEWAL
AUTUMN'S PROMISE

THE CAREGIVER

Families of Honor, Book One

SHELLEY SHEPARD GRAY

AVON

INSPIRE

An Imprint of HarperCollins*Publishers*

ISBN 978-1-61129-445-3

To Gary and Kelley. Just because.

Happiness is the inner joy that can be sought or caught, but never taught or bought.

—Amish proverb

Even when I walk through the darkest valley, I will not be afraid, for you are close beside me.

—Psalm 23:4

THE CAREGIVER

Prologue

Lucy shielded her face when the antique platter crashed to the floor. Though whether she was shielding it from shards of pottery or bracing herself for another sting from Paul's hand, she didn't really know.

Most likely both.

But all her husband did was pull open the screen door. "You are such a disappointment, Lucy," he bit out, each word seething with venom. "Such a disappointment. In every possible way."

Her lip bled as she fought to remain still under his glaring eyes. Prepared herself for another diatribe. Then Paul simply shook his head in disgust and stormed out the kitchen door. It slammed behind him as he bolted down the stairs and strode along the worn path to their barn.

When his footsteps faded, Lucy leaned against the

gleaming counters of her kitchen and willed herself to stop shaking.

Trembling and crying won't help, she sternly urged herself. When Paul came back, he would expect every trace of the bright blue dish cleaned up and the rest of the kitchen to be spotless. With a scant glance at the clock over the screen door, she saw it was a quarter after six.

She had fifteen minutes. Maybe eighteen.

After wiping the blood from her mouth with a dish-cloth, she carefully picked up the pieces of pottery. Tried not to remember her grandmother's expression when she'd presented the serving piece to her and Paul. Her lip quivered. Oh, but her grandmother had been so proud to give her something that had been in their family for four generations.

And Lucy had been proud to receive it. After all, she was the eldest of six children and was marrying well. Paul Troyer was a pillar of their community and had promised that he would be able to help out her brothers and sisters financially.

And now the dish was shattered. Irreparable. Much like her marriage.

She glanced at the clock again. 6:22. *Oh, but time is wasting!* Quickly, Lucy picked up her pace. Putting both knees on the ground, she scanned the floor and snatched up every shard that she could find, only wincing slightly when one of the pieces tore at her thumb.

After hurriedly bandaging her finger so blood wouldn't stain anything, Lucy wiped the floor with a damp cloth. Then she attacked the dishes—the source of Paul's latest discontent. Dinner had been late. She'd been helping her mother with her littlest sister. Lizzie had the flu and was feverish, so Lucy had offered to watch her while her mother went to school to attend Jeremy and Karl's spelling bee program.

But then her mother had run late. Making Lucy return late. And the chicken had gone into the oven at 5:30 instead of 5:15. Paul had been very angry.

She darted a look out the window. Surmising that he was still in the barn, Lucy breathed a sigh of relief. All she had to do was wash the dishes, scrub two pans, and put them all neatly away before he returned. If she did that, everything might still be all right.

She stole another glance at the clock. 6:26.

With the experience of almost two years of marriage, Lucy hurriedly wrapped up the remains of the dinner, then washed and dried each piece of pottery. Sweat ran down the middle of her back as she raced to put each dish away, then ran a cloth over the counters.

Finally, she straightened out the red-and-white tin canisters to the right of the oven. Made sure they were in perfect alignment, not a one out of place.

Only then did she allow herself to breathe a sigh of relief. The kitchen was clean. She darted yet another glance at the clock. 6:34. She had made it.

As she always did, Lucy braced herself to hear Paul's footsteps. Prepared to meet him with a smile . . . as if he hadn't thrown the dinner platter to the floor. As if he hadn't raised his hand to her.

But still the clock ticked . . . and he didn't arrive. Warily,

Lucy peeked out the window. Glanced at the clock. 6:50.

A new set of worries settled in her stomach. To spend so long in the barn wasn't like him. Paul was nothing if not prompt; and she had learned the hard way about the folly of not adhering to his schedule.

Not knowing what else to do, she pulled out a chair. And waited. Another hour passed.

When the sun started to set, Lucy stood and paced. Common sense told her to walk to the barn to check on her husband. But self-preservation warned her. Paul didn't like her to disturb him. He didn't like her to spy on him.

And surely he would not be happy if she went to the barn without him telling her she could. Almost without thought, she rubbed the knot that now was a permanent fixture on her arm. She'd learned that lesson the hard way.

Thirty minutes later, Lucy felt sick to her stomach. It was now almost 8:30, the time Paul liked to read the Bible and discuss his plans for the next day. Surely something was wrong.

Worrying her bottom lip, she slowly opened the screen door and stepped outside. Her heart skipped a beat when she saw Star, their shepherd mix, whining outside the barn door.

"Star?"

The dog barked, then whined some more. Pulled on the rope that hitched him to a post by the barn's entrance.

Lucy started forward. For Star to be still tied up, that was strange indeed. Usually Paul let him loose once he went into the barn to inspect the horses. "Star? Are you okay?" she asked as she freed the dog.

The dog answered by barking again and pawing at the barn's entrance.

Lucy gathered her courage. Prepared herself to meet Paul's barrage of abuse for disturbing him. Or for him to yank at her shoulder for spying.

But the daylight was waning. Lucy didn't know what Paul wanted her to do, but when Star pawed the door again, she opened it and stepped in. Her heart beat wildly. With a cautious, dry swallow, she whispered, "Paul?"

Only the nervous neigh of their horses replied.

She walked in farther, then stopped in shock.

Paul lay at the base of the ladder that led to the barn's loft. She rushed to his side and knelt, Star at her heels. "Paul!" she cried out. "Paul! Paul?"

That's when she noticed his neck was at an odd angle and his eyes were open. Lifeless.

Gingerly, she pressed two fingers to his neck, searching for a pulse. But there wasn't one. Her husband was dead.

Chapter 1

~One year later~

"Lucy? Lucy, you come here this instant."

Paul's voice echoed through their home, practically shaking the rafters. Definitely shaking her nerves. In a panic, she slipped her pencil into the middle of her diary, shut it, then hastily stuffed it in between the wooden slats and into the box springs of their bed.

She got to her feet and went to find her husband.

He stood at the bottom of the steps, his hands on his hips, rage in his eyes.

"Yes, Paul?" she asked, taking care to keep her tone even and calm.

"Where is the bread you made today?"

She rushed past him, careful not to make contact. In the

kitchen, she opened the bread box. "Here," she said, slipping out the fresh loaf. "Would you like a slice?"

Slowly, he shook his head. "Nee."

He turned from her and stomped off, just as she caught her breath. Oh, that had been a close call. She knew what would have happened if she hadn't found the bread . . .

Abruptly, he turned around. "Lucy? Did you make bread for your family, too?"

Her palms began to sweat. What was the right answer? If she chose wrong, Paul would be upset.

She bit her lip.

"Lucy, can you answer me?"

Oh, that tone. So sarcastic and harsh at the same time! Quickly, she rubbed her damp hands on the sides of her dress. Swallowed hard. "I did make bread for them."

Body tense, she waited for him to respond.

A light shone in his eyes as he stepped forward. His hand was raised. Her breath caught.

"Hello? Hel-lo!"

Lucy opened her eyes and stifled a scream. A little girl was staring at her over the top of the seat in front of her. Little by little, the dream faded and her reality set in.

She was on a train.

Not in her kitchen.

And Paul . . . Paul was gone.

The little girl squinted her eyes as she examined Lucy some more. Pretty little eyebrows framed expressive blue eyes. And a petite white *kapp* covered her head.

Lucy finally spoke. "Hello to you."

A broad smile greeted her. "We're Amish, too!"

When Lucy blinked, the girl laughed and pulled on the shirt of the man next to her.

"She's awake, Calvin," the girl chirped. "She's awake and she's starin' right at me."

Slowly, the man turned and faced Lucy, looking at her over the upholstered seats. "I apologize," he murmured, his expression pained. "My sister Katie doesn't always know when to leave others alone. We'll try to not bother you again."

As the haze of sleep floated away, Lucy suddenly realized that they'd both been speaking Pennsylvania Dutch. Right there in the middle of the train.

That was a curious thing. From the time she'd left the train station in Kalamazoo, she'd hardly come across more than a handful of Amish, and they'd been at the station in Chicago.

"I'm Amish," she said. Unnecessarily, to be sure. After all, the little girl had just made that pronouncement.

But instead of pointing that out, the man—who really was too handsome for his own good—had the nerve to wink. "It's enough to make ya smile, ain't it?" he asked, bright blue eyes shining underneath the brim of his black felt hat. "The coach attendant took Katie, my uncle, and me through practically this whole train here, and I didn't spy a single other Plain traveler. Until you. And now . . . here we all are."

Yes, here we all are, she silently repeated to herself—and against her will felt herself slowly falling into a dark void of panic. It seemed no matter how hard she tried, she couldn't seem to have a real conversation with a man.

Paul hadn't only damaged her physically. He'd damaged her self-confidence as well.

When the silence between them turned awkward, the man pointed to the window. Rain splattered angrily against the pane. "You're lucky you've been able to sleep. The storm is a terrible one, for sure."

Lightning flashed in the distance, glowing bright against the dark sky. Lucy nodded. "I fell asleep more than an hour ago. I didn't even realize it was raining."

"Well, I'm not tired at all," the little girl said.

Lucy couldn't help but be charmed by Katie's blue eyes, rosy cheeks, and chatty nature. Oh, she so did enjoy children. Time and again, she'd prayed for God to bless her with a baby. But none had ever come.

"Katie, you might get tired sooner than you think," she warned with a smile. "That's what happened to me. One minute I was looking out the window, and the next I was sound asleep."

"Until we woke you up," the man said, sounding terribly aggrieved.

"I don't mind."

"You should." Looking at his sister, he shook his head in obvious exasperation. "You must learn to mind your manners, Katie."

"But I don't want to sleep. Traveling is too much fun." She squirmed in another direction, then pointed to a man two rows down. "Uncle John says traveling is an adventure not to be missed."

"But if you'll notice, he's also sitting far from you."

"Calvin, you know Uncle John said he was sorry that we couldn't sit three to a seat. He said he was real sad about that."

His tone wry, Calvin said, "Somehow, I doubt that."

As Lucy continued to watch the pair with interest, the man rolled his eyes. "As you can see, my tiny sister here is like a whirling top. Nothing seems to slow her down. It's no wonder my mother asked me to take her with me to Indianapolis. She probably needed a vacation of her own."

He smiled again, but in spite of her best intentions, Lucy wasn't able to relax enough to return his grin. No matter what, it seemed as if Paul was still always with her, judging her reactions to him. To other men. Watching her . . . Little by little, both her family and other members of her community had come to accept that Lucy was far different from the bright, smiling girl she had once been. Of course, most in the community kept their distance— they'd known how Paul had treated her . . . and had chosen to look the other way.

But instead of looking at her strangely, the man seemed amused by Lucy's lack of conversation. "So, I'm guessing you didn't board here in South Bend," he said. "When did you get on?"

"Back in Michigan."

"So you've been traveling for some time—"

"A really long time," Katie interjected.

"I have," she told the child. "Hours and hours. I boarded a different train back in Kalamazoo, then got on this one in Chicago."

"You've had quite an exciting day, then."

She tensed, sure he was teasing her. Finding fault. But then she noticed that his whole demeanor was patient. Kind. Not searching for blunders.

His little sister didn't look timid around him at all.

"*Jah*," she finally said. With effort, Lucy pushed back the unease she felt rushing forward, heating her cheeks. *Just because a man is handsome like Paul, it doesn't mean he's like him inside*, she cautioned herself.

"We haven't traveled by train too often, neither. I must have checked my reservation ten times, I was so worried about boarding the wrong train. You and me, Katie, and my Uncle John will have to stick together then, *jah*?"

For a moment, she was tempted to smile right back and take him up on his offer. But that would be a silly thing to do. Within a few hours the train would stop in Cleveland and she'd never see them again.

So she settled for self-preservation. "*Jah*," she said simply, then turned her head away so she wouldn't see the expression in their eyes.

Obviously misjudging her uneasiness, he cleared his throat. "By the way, I'm Calvin and this, here, is my sister Katie."

"Katie Weaver," his sister corrected.

"And I am Lucy Troyer."

Calvin inclined his head. "Lucy, we are pleased to meet you."

"I as well," she said. Then feeling like a fool again, she turned toward the window and closed her eyes. Though she tried her best to relax, she was finding it next to impossible. She was too aware of his presence. His smile. His easy way of moving.

And the horrible knowledge that once again she was noticing a much too handsome man whom she really knew nothing about. And was accepting his words at face value.

Just as she'd once done with Paul.

As Lucy turned away and closed her eyes, Calvin bit back regret. When he'd first spied her sitting in the row behind them, he'd been thanking his lucky stars. She was a pretty thing. Her hair was the color of dark honey, and her light golden eyes reminded him of the fields outside his kitchen window on an August morning.

But her attitude was curious. With Katie, she seemed relaxed and easy to talk to. With him, however, her manner was different. She'd been skittish. Bordering on rude.

No, that's not quite right, he reflected. Her manner had been more circumspect. Restrained. Actually, it was almost as if she'd been afraid of *him*.

He frowned. Never before in his twenty-six years had a woman looked at him with such apprehension. On the contrary, most seemed to go out of their way to be good company.

He'd always taken that for granted, he supposed. It was what came of being Calvin Weaver, the oldest son of the Weaver family—the biggest landowners in Jacob's Crossing.

As Katie squirmed next to him, he prayed she'd fall asleep soon. "Settle, *shveshtah*," he murmured.

"I'm tryin'. But it's hard to get comfortable."

"Try harder. You're making too much noise."

"You take up too much room." After a pause, she said, "Maybe I could go sit beside Lucy? She hardly takes up half a seat."

"Of course you can't."

Katie's expression turned mutinous. "Why not?"

"Because you can't just go sit next to someone you don't know."

"People do on the train."

Her logic was giving him a headache. "Hush now."

"But—"

He raised an eyebrow.

"Fine." She turned her back to him, and squirmed and fidgeted.

While she did that, Calvin turned his mind back to Lucy.

What, he wondered, had set her off? Had he said something that could be misconstrued? Replaying their brief conversation in his mind, he could think of nothing untoward. Perhaps she just hadn't felt like talking.

After another bout of restlessness, Katie curled up in a ball under a thick blanket and finally stilled.

Peace at last!

Though it was a bad idea, Calvin took the opportunity to pull a worn letter from his jacket's inside pocket. In the relative privacy of his seat, he smoothed out the creases, rubbing his thumb against the folds . . . and over the words he had memorized six weeks ago. But couldn't seem to let go of.

His last letter from Gwen.

There was no reason for him to still have the note. He knew why Gwen had broken up with him. Everyone in Jacob's Crossing knew. She'd fallen in love with one of his friends and had been too full of herself to even tell him in person.

No, she'd written him a letter.

Which he still kept, much to his embarrassment.

Dear Calvin, the letter began. *I fear I must finally be honest with you . . .*

She'd *feared.* "*Finally.*" Each word and phrase hurt him anew. Calvin blinked, then, like an addict, focused on the words again, farther down the page.

Will and I, we can't help our feelings, you see . . .

As the words swam in front of him, he remembered the conversation with his brothers.

"Why don't you go to Indiana for a spell," his youngest brother, Graham, had said. "There's no need for you to witness their courting."

But running away had seemed weak, and he'd told them that.

His brother Loyal had simply laughed. "What does it matter if people think you're weak or strong? All that matters is how you feel. And for the record, I think you have every right to feel betrayed."

"*Jah,*" Graham added. "They went and fell in love right under your nose, Calvin. Get away from here for a week or so. Clear your head."

"Or better yet, take Katie," Loyal added.

"*Katie?*" he'd asked in surprise and, admittedly, with trepidation.

"Yes, that would be a mighty *gut* idea," his youngest brother said. "She's been pestering Mamm something awful these days. Mamm would be terribly grateful if you got her out of her hair for a bit."

But though his brothers' advice made perfect sense—and though his mother had wholeheartedly supported his vacation—Calvin had hemmed and hawed. He'd stayed up many nights and prayed for answers. For the right answers. But the only advice that rang true to him was in his brothers' words.

That there was no shame in being hurt.

So, with his little sister in tow, he'd left Jacob's Crossing and journeyed west to Indianapolis. There, they visited Uncle John, who'd become an *Englischer* when Calvin was just a child.

While in Indianapolis, the three of them visited the city's children's museum and sampled ice cream on park benches. They'd walked city blocks and ridden bicycles. Slowly, Calvin began to feel less depressed about his reasons for being there and had begun to take comfort in the blessings he was given. He admired the tall buildings and the intricately designed gardens. He bought a dozen postcards to show his brothers. And Katie's indefatigable spirit brightened his days.

Just as they were preparing to leave, John surprised the both of them by saying he wanted to accompany them back. "I've been gone for too long. For twenty years; since I was eighteen," he said, speaking of Geauga County and their many relatives.

"We'll be glad to have you near," Calvin had said, but

inside, his mind was spinning. All he'd ever heard was that John had moved away and never looked back. That he'd abandoned all of them with his English ways and his worldly views.

Though, that wasn't true, because, after all, he'd been a mighty good host to him and Katie. Calvin had definitely gotten the impression that he liked his life in Indianapolis. And that he never pined for his old life—or his family.

But perhaps that also wasn't true.

Now, as he looked at Gwen's letter, Calvin forced himself to look to the future. In mere hours, they'd be back in Jacob's Crossing. There, Calvin felt sure he could go back to his old life. If he tried real hard, Calvin was certain he'd be able to tell everyone that Gwen and Will's new affection for each other hardly mattered to him at all.

He knew he needed to throw out Gwen's note and move on, in mind as well as deed.

But, as if his hands acted of their own accord, the paper was folded and neatly slipped back into his pocket. There would be another time. Another, better time.

Twenty minutes later, Katie stretched and sat up. "Can I have a snack now?"

"You just ate, child."

"Almost two hours ago. I'm hungry again."

He sincerely doubted that. Most likely, she was just restless. And eager to pester the woman behind them. "Don'tcha think you should try to fall back to sleep?"

"I can't with the storm. It's thundering something awful." With a mischievous smile, she said, "Calvin, I think some of the Oreos Uncle John gave us would make me feel better."

"All right, then. Sit tight," he murmured, standing up. Unable to help himself, he glanced Lucy's way.

She was watching him, her golden eyes looking like they didn't miss a thing.

"My sister, she needs a snack," he explained.

"So I heard." A slight smile appeared for a second, then vanished like an apparition.

He'd just reached his arms up to grab hold of the fabric handle of his bag overhead when the train rocked.

"Oh!" Lucy said.

Outside, a flash of lightning illuminated the sky. Inside, the row of fluorescent lights flickered. The train rocked again.

Almost losing his balance, Calvin reached for the chrome bar and gripped it hard.

"Calvin! *Gebb acht!*" Katie warned.

"I *am* being careful. Don't worry so," he chided just as the lights flickered again and seemingly gave up the fight, shrouding everyone in darkness.

Beside him, Katie jumped to her feet . . . and Lucy cried out.

Chapter 2

"Katie? Lucy? Are you both all right?" Calvin asked through the shadows.

"I am fine," Lucy replied as embarrassment floated over her. *Oh, honestly!* Where was the woman she used to be? The one who would have looked at this journey as a grand adventure?

Sometimes she scarcely recognized herself. Sudden noises and happenings affected her now. Yet another consequence of her marriage. Belatedly, Lucy realized that the little girl hadn't answered. As she saw Calvin return to his seat through the shadows, she leaned forward and spoke through the gap in the seats. "Katie, are you fine, too?"

Still no answer.

Calvin's voice turned sharper. "Katie?"

"I'm here," the little girl finally answered, her high-pitched voice floating through the space in between them.

Calvin's voice turned firmer. "You need to answer when I call you."

"I was scared."

"Well, there is no need for that," Calvin replied. "I am here."

Lucy smiled to herself as she saw Calvin slip a comforting arm around his sister's shoulders. Turning parental even though he wasn't her parent. Being the oldest of six, she'd certainly done that a time or two. Or two hundred. It was the way of families, she supposed.

At least Amish ones. Older children looked after the younger ones. She vividly remembered rocking one of her brothers to sleep when she was only six. But then, of course, all that changed when she'd married. Paul had refused to let her help out like she used to, saying he needed her at home. After they were married, she'd visited her siblings only in emergencies.

Of course, she'd often been reluctant to leave her house, for fear that her siblings would see her bruises and ask too many questions.

Katie's head popped up over the seat in front of her, interrupting her thoughts. "Lucy, can I come sit with you?"

"You don't want to keep your *bruder* or your uncle company?"

"Uncle John has no room next to him. And Calvin is hard to sit next to. He's too big. You're much smaller."

"She's been talking about changing seats since we met you," Calvin said, turning back toward Lucy. "But don't worry," he added, sounding aggrieved. "I told her to leave you alone."

Since all she could do in the dark was remember her past, Lucy jumped at the chance to have Katie next to her. "Of course you can sit with me, Katie. I'd be happy for the company." And truly, she would.

Without realizing she'd been holding her breath, Lucy exhaled. Everything was going to be all right. She wasn't going to embarrass herself by not being able to control her emotions. And Calvin wasn't going to push her for information about why she was so skittish.

"You're sure you don't mind?" Calvin asked through the shadows.

"Not in the slightest." Even to her ears, she sounded perfectly normal. Yes, she could do this. She could push all her worries and dark memories away.

When would she finally begin to step forward in her life, instead of constantly looking backward?

Lucy hated the burden of feeling the need to look over her shoulder.

Katie jumped out of her seat, then hopped right up next to Lucy as another bolt of lightning illuminated the sky.

"I don't like storms," she said, shivering slightly. "And I 'specially don't like them when we're sittin' on a *trayn*."

"I don't care for storms much, either," Lucy said. "But I've found it easier if I think of thunder and lightning as a game."

"What kind of game?"

"I'll show you," Lucy replied. "Let's listen for the thunder, shall we? If we count one Mississippi, two Mississippi, we'll be able to tell how far away the storm is."

Katie slid a hand into hers. "One Miss-ippi. Two Miss-ippi," she blurted, stumbling over the state's name, making Lucy laugh. When they heard the answering thunder, she gasped. "That was three Miss-ippi! Was that close?"

"Closer than I'd like," Lucy said.

In front of them, Calvin whistled low. "We're right in the thick of this storm." He paused. "I'm afraid things are going to get worse before they get better."

That seemed likely. After all, that was the way things were. The way things always were.

"We are experiencing a minor technical malfunction," a tinny-sounding voice over the loudspeaker suddenly proclaimed. "Please be patient while we do our best to analyze the problem."

A few groaned. More than one person scoffed at the announcement.

Calvin sniggered. "Don't see that there is much to analyze. The lights don't work."

"They're off for good, maybe," Katie proclaimed.

"So, Lucy . . . are you all right now?" Calvin asked. Sounding kind. Almost like he really cared.

With the darkness making one of her senses nearly unneeded, her others became more pronounced. She couldn't help hearing how tentative his voice sounded, like he was afraid of spooking her. Like she was a frightened child or a wounded animal.

Which, of course, she was in many ways. "I'm just fine. I just got a little rattled."

"Ah. Well, that would be easy enough to do."

She clung to the excuse like it was the strongest of lifelines. And pushed herself to sound as confident as she could. They had Katie to keep happy, of course.

"Things will get better soon, I imagine. Before you know it, the lights will flash on again and we'll be right as, uh, rain." He chuckled, obviously enjoying his small joke. "And if we stay in the dark, well, that's okay, too. It's going to take more than a busted electrical system on a train to get me down."

"Or me," Katie said happily.

"Or me," Lucy said, feeling like she should join in, though she felt like a liar. After all, when was the last time she'd felt such confidence? "Yes, I'm sure everything will improve momentarily," she fibbed, pretending her most pressing problem was a power outage.

"We'll get through this, I know it," he said, obviously doing his best to get his sister settled. "Everything seems off balance, but all we can do is make the best of things."

Make the best of things. Oh, yes, she'd heard that advice before. It was what her mother had told her time and again during her first year of marriage.

"Paul is your husband," she'd say. *"You have promised to love and honor him."*

Just once Lucy had wanted to ask why Paul hadn't been expected to love or honor her.

After two years of marriage, Lucy had learned to only trust herself. Paul had become increasingly harder to please, and had made no secret of the fact. Most everyone around her, though they obviously felt sorry for her, had offered no support.

Because, of course, he was her husband.

Then that one fateful evening—when he'd yelled at her for not having his supper ready on time and had thrown her grandmother's platter to the floor—everything had changed.

She flinched as she recalled her nervousness when going to check on him in the barn. Her mouth went dry as she remembered the awkward way in which his neck had set after his fall from the ladder.

And guilt flowed as she realized once again that it had been relief that she'd felt when she'd realized he was dead.

Oh, yes. She'd been mighty relieved.

Now, a year later, Lucy knew it was time to make some changes. She liked what Calvin said—to *make the best of things*. Perhaps she should finally learn to start making the best of things. There was comfort in optimism, she supposed.

Next to her, Katie was cuddled up, dozing off again. She closed her eyes and concentrated on the little girl's sweet smell, all soap and starch.

Around them, the other passengers shifted and talked. Much of the conversations that floated around them sounded like hers and Calvin's. People didn't want to be afraid but were concerned about the storm.

A buzzing rose to a crescendo, then faded. Moments later, with another flicker, the lights came on again.

Cheers erupted.

Lucy glanced Calvin's way and caught his smile.

When their eyes met, she felt a pull toward him. Strong enough to make her wish she had more confidence. Wish she wasn't so damaged.

As a few people walked by them, he murmured, "Since Katie's asleep, would you mind terribly if I got up for a bit and went with my uncle to the dining car?"

"Of course not."

For another moment, she met his gaze. Again, a spark seemed to fly between them. "I promise, I didn't intend to saddle *you* with her."

"You haven't. "

"She's a girl who is used to getting her way." He frowned slightly. "She's spoiled, I think."

"Maybe she's just lucky."

It was obvious that he still felt hesitant about leaving her with Katie. But instead of pushing her, he stood up. "I'll see you in a bit, then."

When he disappeared down the narrow aisle, Lucy felt her spirits lift just thinking of his words, of him. He was a big man, a man obviously used to hard physical labor. Most likely a farmer.

His "snack" would probably be a full meal for her.

Able to relax more, now that she wasn't so disturbed by his presence, Lucy turned her thoughts to the reason for her trip: to help her cousin Mattie through four weeks of chemotherapy treatments.

Oh, Mattie. She was so thankful for her. When Paul died, her cousin had come and stayed with her for a few weeks . . . and had listened stoically when, little by little, Lucy had poured out her grief and all the pain that she'd been storing for two years.

Mattie hadn't said a word—had only listened and hugged

her tight when Lucy finally admitted the guilt she felt for not mourning his loss more. But, perhaps, she'd already mourned enough. For too many months, she'd mourned the loss of all her hopes.

For that, Lucy knew she would do just about anything to help her cousin. Mattie's parents were older than hers. And her mother, though always meaning well, seemed to be easily distracted. Instead of working with Mattie to handle the stress of her surgery and cancer treatments, she would focus on the small things, such as what color dress Mattie should wear to her appointments.

At least, that's what Mattie had said.

Mattie had written that, often, after her mastectomy, she'd found herself comforting her mother instead of the other way around. Lucy sincerely hoped Mattie would find her presence a help, and that she would learn to lean on her during her month's stay.

Yes, that's what she would do. She would concentrate only on Mattie's needs. That would enable her to keep her mind off her own pain and start to move on.

Above her head, the lights hummed; flickered off, then on again. Another buzz sounded, and Lucy held her breath—anticipating the worst—but the lights seemed to hold. Everyone around her breathed sighs of relief.

But scant ten seconds later, the lights shut off again. Turning Lucy's world small. Now she had only her memories to keep her company, and the feeling of the train going too fast.

And in spite of herself, she wished for Calvin to be sitting by her side. Chatting, smiling . . . making her smile.

Ah. Obviously he had affected her far more than she'd thought.

Mattie Lapp was truly grateful for the hospital van that carried her and her mother to and from the medical center. Charlie, the driver, was a man about her parents' age who seemed to take most everything in stride. That was helpful, since her mother most definitely did not.

As they sat side by side in the second row of the van, looking out the windows, Mattie did her best to stay relaxed and calm while her mother fidgeted and fussed. Wrung her hands and voiced every concern that popped in her head. And, as was her norm, a lot of concerns popped into her head.

"Mattie, do you remember what the *doktah* said he would check today?"

"The usual things, I suppose. He'll take blood and check my incisions. He said sometimes the stitches are slow to heal."

"Do you think yours are healing?"

Mattie wasn't altogether sure. Ever since she'd left the doctor's office last week, she hadn't wanted to look in the mirror again. Hadn't wanted to see the spot where they'd removed the majority of her left breast. Hadn't wanted to see how she was now scarred and ugly.

It bothered her far more than it should, perhaps. But, just the same, that was the way she felt.

"Mattie, you are healing, *jah?*" her mother asked a bit louder.

Mattie could feel her cheeks heat. What had happened

to her was personal and private, and she surely did not like discussing her body parts so openly. "I think so, Mamm."

"But you're not certain?"

"It's only been two weeks. Plus that's something only the doctors can know for sure, *jah*?"

"Maybe."

Inwardly, Mattie seethed. Though she knew her mother's questions were asked with the best of intentions, and she knew her mother gave up much of her day to accompany her to the appointments, she was eager to have Lucy with her instead. Lucy, with her soft-spoken ways and dry sense of humor, would make even the hardest appointments more manageable.

And just as importantly, she could sit for hours without talking. And that would give Mattie some peace at last.

"I, for one, will be anxious for you to get another scan. I want to make sure they removed all of the cancer."

"They think they did."

"And he thinks you are healing all right?" she asked anxiously. *Again*.

Oh, but her mother tried her patience like no other. "He said I was healing just fine last week, *Muddar*."

"Then I'm sure you are, dear." As her mother mumbled something about scar tissue, and then somehow went on to discuss their dinner menu, Mattie leaned her head back against the beige vinyl seat and swallowed hard.

She'd squinted at her image in the mirror in the cool air of the exam room a week earlier, her doctor standing right next to her, pointing out where the incisions were healing. It had taken every bit of self-control she had to stand tall and straight and look directly . . . at her body, which looked so unfamiliar now.

To her, the sides of her chest looked broken and mismatched. Her right looked like herself, the left was now mottled with angry red scars. And flat, of course. Forever now, she would not have the figure she used to. There would be no reconstructive surgery for her like so many *Englischers* received.

"And then you will start *chemo-ther-apy* next week, ain't so?" her mother asked, stumbling over the unfamiliar word.

"Yes. Lucy will get here, and then next Monday we will begin that."

Her mother wrung her hands again. "I am so grateful for your cousin. Lucy's visit is going to be a blessing for all of us."

"Yes."

"We should be giving thanks for her, Mattie."

"I have been giving thanks for Lucy. Of course I have."

But something in her voice must have not rung true, because her mother narrowed her eyes a bit and examined her more fully. Mattie did her best to look wide-eyed and relaxed under the inspection. But in truth, she felt as if her mother had suddenly located every flaw in her personality.

And Mattie knew there were many. And one, in particular, was most difficult to acknowledge. And that was the painful realization that her faith was not near as solid as she had imagined.

All her life Mattie had found comfort in the Lord's presence. She'd always felt that she'd done her best to be a person she could be proud of, a person who others respected and admired.

As long as she could remember, she'd always done what she was supposed to. She'd been a dutiful daughter. She'd tried hard in school, had tried not to gossip, and lived by the rules of the *Ordnung*. And every night, without fail, she prayed.

She praised God for her many gifts. She gave thanks for her joys and for her family.

So why—at twenty-two years of age—did she get cancer?

That hardly seemed fair.

And though her mother and father spoke, mostly in platitudes, about how no one can know God's will, and how He has a plan for each person . . . for the first time in her life, Mattie wasn't sure she believed that.

Which was, of course, a terrible thing to admit.

"Mattie, we are almost at the medical center," her mother said brightly, as if they were on their way to a county fair. "Perhaps afterward, we could go to the ice cream store and have a treat? Or maybe even to Bob Evans?"

"Yes. That would be nice," Mattie said. Usually, her thoughts about that home-churned vanilla ice cream got her through the difficult examinations.

But today, the treat seemed like a too-small consolation for what was sure to be an uncomfortable appointment and a too-long journey to get there and back.

"Then we'll head back to Jacob's Crossing."

"I will be ready to go home," Mattie answered with far more emotion. She would be very ready to escape to the privacy of her room and relax and sleep. Once again, she wished that the medical center was not so far away. That she didn't have to wait for the driver, and pay him for his time. That her mother—who meant so well, but was so irritating—hadn't made Mattie's cancer the center of her world.

All of it completely exhausted her.

Her mother's cheeks bloomed. "I was going to wait, but I found I cannot keep my secret any longer."

"Secret?"

"A group of us will be getting together at Joanne Knepp's home to make fried pies for you. Mrs. Knepp wants you to come, too."

Mattie's head jolted back. "But, Mamm, I thought you agreed I should go home and rest."

"Daughter, trust me. All the ladies will not expect you to be doing cartwheels," her mother chided, as if Mattie didn't know her mind. "No one expects you to stand on your feet and cook, either. But you could sit on the couch and chat with us, don't you think?"

Mattie sighed. "You know how these appointments wear me out . . ."

"Yes, but seeing some fresh faces and chatting in their company shouldn't be a problem."

Before Mattie could comment, her mother patted her hand. "More likely, their companionship and heartfelt prayers will be just the cure you need."

Mattie felt the bottom fall out of her stomach. The last

thing she wanted was to sit with all of her mother's friends and pretend that she was perfectly fine.

Because even though her body had been healing, her mind seemed to be going down a different path.

And it was toward a terribly dark place.

Chapter 3

After Calvin returned, he stood in the aisle chatting with Lucy over a sleepy Katie. They were whispering; and though hunching down, he could hardly hear Lucy. After she'd repeated the same phrase three times, Calvin had had enough.

He picked up Katie and carefully laid her over their seats.

With bleary eyes, Katie looked around in confusion. "Sleep now, sister," Calvin murmured. "I'll be right behind ya."

When her body relaxed and her eyes drifted closed, he finally took a place next to Lucy.

"This is much better," he said. "My back was going to cramp into a dozen knots if I had to stoop the way I was for much longer."

"I'm surprised it hasn't already," she teased.

Her jest surprised him, and encouraged him as well. She was one of the most circumspect women he'd ever met. Lucy seemed unusually possessive over her words—guarding each one close to her heart before giving it up to him.

But perhaps that wasn't true? She'd had no trouble amusing Katie when they listened for thunder . . . No, her skittishness seemed to be directed only his way.

Once again, he wondered why.

"I have to say, I'm mighty impressed with your sister. She seems to be able to sleep through most anything."

"My parents would call that a blessing," he replied. "She's a late-in-life babe. Born seventeen years after my youngest brother, Graham."

To his pleasure, she chuckled. "I imagine she was quite a surprise."

"Oh, that is putting it mildly." Lowering his voice, he said, "I have to admit that my brothers and I were a bit mystified by her appearance in our lives. We never imagined our parents were still, uh, enjoying the marriage bed."

Her eyes widened.

And he wished he had a sock to stuff in his mouth. "I am sorry. Sometimes I say things I shouldn't."

Though her pretty cheeks turned pink, she shook her head. "Don't apologize. I'm one of six children. My sisters and I have had that same conversation. I suppose some marriages are like that."

Her last phrase was confusing. Calvin was going to ask her to clarify it, but the engine rattled again—and, in spite of his best intentions to act calm and assured, he jumped in alarm. He didn't like things that were out of his control, and the goings-on of the giant train were certainly that. Now the faint scent of gasoline flowed though their car.

He'd followed an attendant with a flashlight when the lights had gone out in the dining car. Though most people had seemed determined to make the best of things and had declared they were fine with the battery-powered candles on the tables, he was not. He felt too out of control. Too out of his element. The motion of the train in the dark felt like the carnival ride he'd tried when his parents had taken them to the county fair when he was twelve.

Though he'd laughed like his brothers, his stomach had been in knots until he'd put his feet back on the ground. He liked things he could control.

And if he couldn't control them, he at least liked to be able to see what was going on.

He'd felt too unsettled . . . and too concerned about his unexpected companion on the train. As quickly as he could, he had finished his cold roast beef sandwich and asked for help getting back to his seat.

And now he was sitting next to Lucy. Through the shadows, he felt her body tense as their silence lengthened.

"Did you find something to eat?"

The question didn't matter, but the effort did, he supposed. "*Jah*. Though I paid too much for it, I suppose."

"I found that to be true when I bought a sandwich on my first train."

Struggling to continue their stilted conversation, he said, "When I traveled west, I brought several sandwiches with me. There was no way I could do that this time, not since we all went to a horse auction first before boarding the train."

A beep and buzz overhead made Lucy jump. "Easy, now," he murmured. "We're safe."

The lights flickered once, twice, then eventually clicked on for good.

Lucy exhaled. "At last!"

He smiled at her. "Ah, Lucy Troyer. It is *gut* to see you again."

"Indeed," she said, her lips curving slightly.

Twenty minutes later, the strange whirring noise grew louder. With a jerk, the train careened forward, pushing many people up from their seats—and causing half a dozen bags to fall out of the overhead bins.

As his backpack and her tote crashed to the floor beside him, then slid down the aisle, Calvin jumped up to retrieve them. But of course, right then the train jerked and rocked. And the lights went out again.

"Calvin?" Katie called out.

"Everything's okay," he said. "I'll be right there. I just have to pick up our things," he explained . . . just as the car wobbled on the tracks.

Worried cries echoed throughout the car as the screech of brakes pierced the air, followed by yet another jerk as, it seemed, the engineer struggled for control.

And Calvin attempted the same, grabbing for the edge of a seat to situate himself. Then, with a sputter and a last dying gasp, the train gave up its battle. Below their feet, a thousand gears screeched and then, with a loud, exuberant sigh, jerked to a stop again.

Bringing yet another batch of luggage, books, umbrellas, and jackets down.

Calvin held on tight as he was pummeled. Something heavy with a sharp edge knocked his head; another item ripped his shirt. *"Umph,"* he grunted.

"Calvin?" Katie asked, her voice tinged with fear. "Calvin? Are you all right?"

He was not. His arm stung, and his forehead felt like it had been introduced to the wrong end of a frying pan.

But that was surely not something he was going to admit so openly. In the dim shadows, he spied their things. With a grunt, he picked up his backpack and little Katie's pink tote. Spying a notebook near his feet that looked to have fallen out of Lucy's bag, he picked it up, then hastily stuffed it into his things. When things were calmer, he'd sort out whose items were whose.

"I've got Katie," Lucy called out. "Come sit with us."

More grateful than ever for Lucy, Calvin trudged back to his seat as an attendant came into the car holding a portable lantern so everyone could get settled.

"Remind me not to do something so foolhardy again," he murmured as he gingerly sat back down. Then he turned to his sister, who was perched on Lucy's lap. "Are you okay?"

Eyes wide, she nodded.

Well, that was not like her at all. Usually she chirped like a magpie. Over Katie's head he met Lucy's gaze. "Is she hurt?"

"I think she is just scared." Her voice caught. "But, Calvin, I fear you're bleeding."

He held up his arm and inspected it. "Where? What can you see?"

"I don't see much on your arm, but your forehead is another story," she murmured as she pulled a tissue from a pocket in her dress.

"There's blood on your shirt, Calvin," Katie murmured. "You're hurt bad. We should go tell Uncle John."

Calvin laughed. "I'm too old to go running to my uncle, Katie. I'm sure this is nothing to fret about, anyway. Heads bleed a lot when they're cut. I'll be right as rain soon," he said, hoping he sounded more sure than he felt.

Though his whole body felt like he'd been thrown from a horse, Calvin twisted and looked outside beyond the girls, craning his neck in what he knew was a futile attempt to see what problem had occurred. Of course he saw nothing.

"I wonder where we are," Lucy said.

"I truly have no idea."

"What do you think this means?" the woman in front of them asked. "Do you think we'll all have to disembark?"

"Your guess is as good as mine," he said. "I've never heard of such a thing happening."

Calvin looked around at the other people doing much the same as he—peering out with worried expressions—and found his uncle. "John, do ya know where we are?"

"Near Toledo, I think. My guess is twenty miles out."

"So we're nowhere near the train station." Leaning toward Lucy, Calvin said drily, "I fear things still aren't getting any better."

To his pleasure, he felt her muscles relax next to him,

and Lucy said, "Now we can only hope they don't get much worse."

Causing Calvin to smile, right there in the dim light.

Minutes later, Katie pressed her lips to Lucy's ear. "I have to go to the bathroom," Katie whispered, but it was loud enough to make Lucy's ear ring. "What should I do?"

"Wait."

She squirmed. "But, Lucy, I don't think I can wait *verra* long."

In spite of the situation, Lucy found herself chuckling. *Of course*, Katie would have such a normal problem in the middle of such an abnormal situation. It was how *kinner* were! For a moment, she closed her eyes and gave thanks to the Lord for bringing Katie and her brother into her life.

If she had still been traveling alone, too afraid to speak to anyone, the situation would be unbearable.

"Lucy?" Katie whispered, her voice impatient as she squirmed. "What should we do? I've *gotta* go."

Lucy couldn't help but notice that Katie had now looped her into the problem. "I think *we* should be patient for a little bit longer, dear. Our attendant should let us know what is happening any moment."

"But—"

"Enough, Katie," Calvin said sharply.

Lucy squeezed the little girl's shoulders. "If no one comes in five minutes, I'll walk you down."

"Promise?"

"Of course," she replied, though she hoped it wouldn't come to that. Walking through the dim light with a child while stepping over fallen luggage and other personal items would be quite an obstacle course.

Luckily, right then, their attendant stepped into the train car, a flashlight beaming in his hand.

Immediately, everyone halted their conversations and looked his way.

"Quiet! Quiet, please." After he cleared his throat, he spoke again. "I regret to inform you all that due to circumstances beyond our control, we will have to unload the train."

"What happened?" Katie's Uncle John called out, his deep voice full of authority.

"The engineer has not informed me," the attendant replied primly.

"Well, why not?" another man called out.

Lucy leaned forward to hear the answer. But instead of responding to the question, the attendant turned forceful. "Please, everyone, remain calm. I know some of you have experienced some injuries, and others are terribly shaken up. The engineer has called ahead and requested medical assistance."

As various people murmured about their slight injuries, Lucy noticed that Calvin merely sat silently—as if his forehead weren't bleeding. "At the moment, we are attempting to turn on our emergency power source. With any luck, the lights will flicker on in a few moments."

A few moments later, the attendant spoke again. "Buses have arrived," he proclaimed. "We will unload and take you to Toledo. There, we will do our best to rebook all of you in a timely fashion. For everyone's safety, please gather your items and move forward."

Around her people groaned but were fairly obedient as they gathered their belongings.

Katie scrambled to her feet. "Oh, I hope we can hurry! I've *really* gotta go."

"We'll do our best," Lucy promised with a wink in Calvin's direction as they stepped into the aisle.

Calvin took his sister's hand. "You hold my hand until I find you a bathroom. I don't want to lose you."

"I won't let go," Katie promised, her tone of voice high and excited. Just as if they were on a wonderful-*gut* adventure.

Doing her best to look eager for the adventure, too, Lucy smiled Katie's way as she joined the line. They'd taken about five steps when she realized that she'd been so preoccupied with Katie that she'd completely forgotten her quilt bag. It was still on her seat. She stepped to the side.

"Lucy?" Calvin asked over his shoulder.

"I forgot my bag. You go ahead in line and then I'll catch up."

Katie's eyes widened. "But what if we lose ya?"

"You won't," Lucy promised. "We're all going to the same place."

"Should we wait for you?"

"*Now* you want to wait?" Calvin asked his sister. "After doing nothing but complaining about needing to visit the restroom? I think not. Lucy, we'll see you on the bus."

Lucy waved to Katie. "I'll be right behind you two."

Katie bit her lip. "But—"

Their uncle stepped in. "Come now, Katie. You are

holding up the line. And you need to find a washroom, A.S.A.P."

Looking over her shoulder one last time, Katie gave Lucy a little wave, then obediently turned and walked forward. Moments later, they were off the train.

It took Lucy quite some time to backtrack to her seat. After she did, she slipped the handles of her bag over her arm and waited for another break in line.

But the attendant's voice had gotten more shrill. And whether it was that or the thunderstorm outside, the line of people began to jostle even more. Tension rose in her as she looked from one face to the next.

The moment that she stepped out of the train car, rain pattered against her skin. "Come along," another train employee called out, his face and voice barely visible under all of his rain gear.

Lucy looked for Calvin and Katie. Surely they were out of the restroom by now? But every time she paused, the man behind almost bumped into her.

The attendant was running out of patience. "Don't hold up the line," he called out. "Miss, go straight to the closest bus."

"I will," she said politely. "However, I'm just looking for the man I was sitting next to—"

"You'll see him in Toledo. Board. Now."

Lucy didn't see Calvin anywhere. As the rain soaked her skin, and she made the quick jaunt to the bus's open door, she continually looked around for Calvin and Katie.

No sign of them. Not on her bus. Not anywhere outside.

"Take a seat, please," the bus driver called out.

There seemed to be only one empty seat. At the back, next to a little five-year-old boy who was holding a teddy bear. Slowly, she sat down next to him.

Seconds later, the front doors to the bus closed and they were off again. Driving through the night toward the lights of Toledo.

All around her were the sights and sounds of irritable, tired, soaked-to-the-skin people.

And Lucy learned that there was, indeed, something far worse than sitting next to the only Amish man on the train. It was sitting on the bus . . . and having him be nowhere in sight.

Chapter 4

Calvin couldn't believe he'd lost Lucy. He had watched with dismay when she pulled herself out of the line and backtracked to her seat. He was going to wait for her, but the attendant wanted none of that—and they needed to find a bathroom for Katie.

"Keep forward, sir," the attendant had cautioned. "Don't disrupt the process."

Now, as he sat in the dark and could see faint traces of dawn peeking over the horizon, the bus sped down the highway—and he hoped Lucy was all right and had, indeed, gotten on the other transport to Toledo.

But of course, why wouldn't she have?

He needed only a second to realize why he was worried. Because she seemed so fragile, that was why. He didn't know much about what led people to do the things they did, but even he could tell that something had happened in Lucy's past that made her see the world in a cautious, tentative way.

Right then and there, he vowed to at least help her get to where she was going. That would be the kind thing to do.

Reaching into his backpack, he pulled out the book he'd found and opened up the front cover. "Lucy Troyer" was printed neatly on the inside cover. After slipping it back in his backpack, he amended his vow. He needed to help her get to her destination and give her back her book. Yes, that was the least he could do.

It had been years since John Weaver had been on a bus. Almost twenty. Once he'd gotten his driver's license, he'd sworn to himself that he'd never get on the bus again. Well, not if he could help it.

Smelling the sweet, thick odor of sanitizer mixed with exhaust fumes made him feel sick. Because it all reminded him of his journey from Jacob's Crossing to Indy—and how scared and awkward he'd been.

Now, as the overhead lights dimmed, and he'd assured himself that his niece and nephew were doing as well as possible, John went back to what had been occupying his mind for the majority of the trip.

The fact that he was finally returning to Jacob's Crossing.

When he'd left the order at eighteen, he'd been a far different person. His temper had been lightning quick, and the chip he'd carried on his shoulder had been big and unruly. Almost the size of a boulder, he thought wryly.

But he'd felt justified.

His older brother had been the perfect son. He, on the other hand, had been the disappointment.

His parents had made sure to tell him that on a daily basis. "Be more like Jacob," they'd said. "Try harder."

They'd never attempted to understand his point of view—that no matter how hard he'd try, he'd never be the paragon that was Jacob.

And so he'd decided to leave.

For months, he'd put aside money and planned his future. But of course, he'd been beyond naïve. All he'd really planned was an escape, not a life.

But now that he was older, he found himself looking back on that confusing time with more than a bit of nostalgia. He'd taken the bus to Indianapolis because living in a different state had felt as daring as other boys might have felt about a journey to Africa or the Middle East. Soon after he arrived, he'd found a room in a rundown boardinghouse and had gotten a job washing dishes in an Italian restaurant.

But surely God had been looking out for him. The people who owned the restaurant were good folks and had taken him under their wing.

And of course, so had their daughter, Angela.

He closed his eyes, preferring to block out the present and focus on the past: Angela had long black hair and dark eyes. She lined those eyes with black eyeliner and wore red lipstick. Her skirts were form-fitting and her manner suggestive—and full of promises he'd only dreamed about. From the moment he'd met her, he was toast. She'd smile and flirt and was loud and loving and everything he'd never known before.

Barely a year later, they'd married.

Unable to stop himself, he recalled their first months together. He'd lived in a haze of newlywed bliss. Food hardly mattered to him. Actually, not much had mattered to him except her lips, he realized with some embarrassment.

During those days, he'd pushed away all thoughts about his past and his family. Concentrated on being a husband and provider. Ironically, he'd concentrated on being the kind of man his parents would have been proud of. The kind of man Jacob was.

And he'd thought he'd succeeded—until he found Angela with another man.

John's eyes popped open. Remembering his dismay. Their arguments. Angela's disdain of his "country" ideals.

The humiliation of knowing that he was the first person in his family to ever divorce.

And that's when he also realized that everything his parents said had been true. He wasn't good enough, and he never would be.

That pain felt as fresh as ever. Even now, almost twenty years later. Which showed him that even after all this time, he was still the same confused boy he'd always been.

Here he was, going back to Jacob's Crossing—and he didn't have a clue about what he was going to do there.

Chapter 5

The Toledo train station was overflowing with emergency personnel, bus managers, and dozens of tired, cranky people.

As soon as Lucy exited the bus, she looked for Calvin and Katie. Even their uncle. But instead of seeing Calvin's black hat or hearing Katie's constant chatter, all she saw was a sea of *Englischers*. Taken off guard, she froze.

"Go to your right, miss." A uniformed man pointed impatiently. "You're holding up the line. We don't have all day."

"Sorry," Lucy murmured as she walked in the direction he indicated, but still craned her neck, hoping against hope that she would suddenly spot Calvin and his sister. But no matter how hard she looked, they were not to be found.

She chewed on her bottom lip as her line inched forward.

Conversations spun in the air around her, but she paid them no mind. Instead, all she was able to think about was how disappointed she was not to see any of the Weavers.

Well, if she was being honest with herself, Lucy knew she wasn't looking for all the Weavers. Though Katie was an adorable child and his uncle seemed terribly kind, Lucy was upset not to see Calvin. She felt his absence like a physical thing, like he'd taken her coat and she now felt the rain and cold all the more.

She couldn't understand why. She usually did everything she could to stay away from contact with men. Until she'd met Calvin, she would have never guessed she would actually enjoy another man's company.

Lucy shook her head, trying to snap out of it. Again a uniformed man directed her to another line, this one in front of a ticket booth. "How will I board my train to Cleveland?" she asked. "What time does it leave?"

He rolled his eyes. "It depends which train we can get you on."

"But—"

"Do you still have your original ticket?" he snapped.

His rude tone rattled her. Hastily, Lucy opened her bag. "*Jah*. It's right—"

"I don't need to see it this minute," he interrupted. "Just show it to the agent at the ticket window and she'll get you on the next available train out of here."

"The one going to Cleveland?" Really, she couldn't understand his directions. Or why he insisted on speaking so fast . . .

"Yes."

"Oh. All right, then. Thank you." She tried to smile, but the gesture, like her words, seemed to be a waste. The man had already started barking orders at the person behind her.

Strangers pushed ahead, their belongings jostling her, making her feel even more ill at ease. Her hair and *kapp* were still damp, and she felt exposed standing by herself. Inch by inch, her line moved. She hitched her quilt bag up higher on her shoulder and stepped forward. All of a sudden, she felt overly warm in her wool cloak.

The station was hot and humid. Though thunder and lightning weren't flashing anymore, a light rain still pattered the windows. Moisture permeated the lobby. The light musty smell of mildew and damp clothes made her sneeze.

After a moment, she stepped forward again. Shifting her quilt bag so she could open it, Lucy reached in and checked for her wallet.

But instead of having to shuffle through the contents of the bag like she usually did, it seemed rather empty. She sighed in relief when she found her wallet.

But then Lucy's stomach knotted.

Her diary was missing. Inside the leather cover, she'd scrawled pages and pages of her innermost feelings. All her anger and fear and worries. And now it was in someone else's hands—just waiting to be opened and read.

Her words, bare and exposed. Penned for anyone to see.

Calvin bit back a burst of frustration as he left the make-shift nurses' station in the back of the terminal. No matter how hard he'd argued, the train personnel hadn't allowed him to do anything but get examined by the nurse the moment he'd gotten off the bus.

"It's policy, sir," a representative from the train had said while he took Calvin's name and address. "I'm sure you understand. We don't want to get sued."

Sued? He didn't understand that reasoning at all. "I don't want to sue anyone. I just want to be on my way."

"In due time. Go take a seat."

After telling John that they'd meet up with him when he was finished, Calvin took Katie's hand and led her to the small grouping of chairs.

After twenty minutes, he was called over to a curtained area, Katie in tow.

"Your forehead needs stitches," the nurse murmured after she cleaned his wound.

"Are you sure?"

"I'm positive, Mr. Weaver," she said briskly, looking at his form. "Now close your eyes, and I'll try to make this as painless and quick as possible."

Beside him, Katie hopped to her feet and inched closer.

"Katie, this might make you squeamish. Why don't you go back to our chairs?"

"Nuh-uh. I'm standing here. I want to see the nurse sew you up."

"I guess this is exciting, ain't it?" he asked, sharing a grin with the nurse.

"Loyal and Graham are gonna be jealous," she said.

"And who are they?" the nurse asked kindly as she gave him a shot.

"They're my other big brothers," Katie answered. "I've got three of them. And an uncle, too."

The nurse shared a smile with Calvin as she pulled on latex gloves. "I'll make the stitches as small as possible, Mr. Weaver."

"Makes no difference to me," he said. "My nose is already crooked."

"Calvin broke his nose four years ago," Katie explained helpfully.

"Hush, child," he said as the nurse began to stitch.

Amazingly, Katie stayed quiet and still beside him. Only slipping her hand into his as the nurse got to work.

"You might want to get an X-ray for your swollen wrist when you get home," the nurse said when she finished and pulled off her gloves. "I don't think it's more than a minor sprain, but sometimes you just can't be sure."

"If it gets worse, I'll do that," he promised.

"And keep the stitches clean. They can be removed in about a week."

He was already guiding Katie toward the door. "All right."

"And Mr. Weaver . . ."

Impatiently, he looked at the nurse. "Yes?"

"I hope you get home soon," she said with a smile.

Her good wishes embarrassed him. "Thank you," he said. "And I thank you for your assistance as well."

The nurse beamed. "You're welcome. Send the next person over on your way out, please."

Calvin told the teenager sitting by the door to go back, then entered the wide-open space of the terminal. Immediately, he was besieged by noise. "Hold my hand again, Katie."

Staring at the throng of people, Katie slipped her hand in his without a word.

At least two hundred people were in the enclosure. Some milled around, others were standing in long lines. Instead of being irritated by the crowd, he was relieved. If there were this many people, Lucy had to be around somewhere. "Let's look for Uncle John now."

Katie nodded. "And Lucy, too."

"Yes, and Lucy, too, of course," he replied.

On a mission, Calvin practically stomped to the closest line of people and began to scan faces for John or Lucy. They located John easily.

"Might as well cool your heels for a bit," John said when they got to his side. "Things are a disorganized mess. We're sure to be here for a while."

But Calvin knew he wasn't going to be able to do anything until he located Lucy. "Katie, stay here, wouldja? I'm going to go look for Lucy." Quickly, he turned away before she could even think about arguing.

Walking along the second line, Calvin searched the faces. Some people met his gaze, others were only looking directly forward. Then he saw her. There, near the front, was a terribly innocent-looking Amish woman, standing straight and as tall as her small frame would allow.

Her cheeks were pale and her light golden eyes looked luminescent as she stared around with obvious distress. He waved as he marched up to her. "Lucy."

Immediately she turned in his direction, and her worried expression eased. "Calvin. Praise God! I was beginning to think I would never see you again."

"They made me get seen by the nurse. "

She pointed to his head. "I see you did need stitches."

"Indeed I did." He smiled, so glad they had connected again.

A woman behind Lucy glared at him. "You're not going to cut in line are you?"

"No. I'm just talking to my friend."

"Talk to her later," she said. "You're slowing down the line."

Calvin didn't think that was the case, but he was in no hurry to argue. "Lucy, John and Katie are waiting in the seating area. Will you look for us when you get done?"

She looked at the woman behind her, then at him. After a second's pause, she picked up her quilt bag and stepped out of line. "I'll take my place at the back with you. Now that I found you, I don't want to be alone."

As she heard her words out loud, her eyes widened in obvious embarrassment. "I . . . I mean, I'd rather not stand by myself here in the terminal if I don't have to," she added in a rush, practically stumbling over her words. "Since, you know, we are all traveling to Cleveland."

"I knew what you meant. I feel the same way," he murmured. And realized right then and there that he meant *every* word he said.

Twenty minutes later, Calvin left the ticket agent's booth feeling no more at ease than he had since the power had gone off in the train. His patience was certainly wearing thin.

But just as he was ready to share his frustration with Lucy, he noticed the lines of worry etched on her forehead. She was already stressed enough. He didn't need to add to that by complaining. It was time to get a new attitude, and fast.

Calvin resolved to try to help Lucy. Surely it was the least he could do . . . he hated the thought of someone hurting her. Of treating her tender feelings roughly.

Of stamping out the thread of spunk that he had a good feeling lurked within her.

"I can't believe our next train doesn't leave for six more hours," he said as he joined their small group.

"When the ticket agent told me the time, I questioned her as well," John said. "But lots of the trains are full. This was the first available. "

Pure dismay crossed Lucy's features. "We seem to be destined to run into troubles."

"It does seem that way." With a weary smile, he said, "Once again, I suppose we should make the best of things. There has to be a reason all this is happening."

Looking around the train depot, which was little more than a large room with a few ticket windows and an area to await the trains, Lucy frowned. "I wonder what I should do."

He latched on to that pronoun. "Do you wish to be on your own now?"

"No. I mean, I like keeping company with you all. If you don't mind me tagging along." She nibbled her bottom lip. "Or perhaps you three have other things to do?"

"I don't." Teasing, he crossed his arms and looked at his sister. "Katie, do you?"

She giggled as she swung her legs and shook her head. "Nope."

John held up a book. "I do. I'm happy to sit here and read or maybe get on my laptop. But you three feel free to explore the city."

Unable to stop himself, he reached out and patted her arm. "Lucy, I'm afraid you're stuck with us." Holding out three vouchers, he handed Lucy one. "I almost forgot—we did receive these, and found out that they're offering special sit-down meals at the restaurant across the way. The attendant told me the food was actually pretty tasty. How about we go eat there and decide what to do?"

Katie's smile grew a mile wide. "I want to do that. I'm really hungry."

Getting to her feet, Lucy chuckled. "Somehow I thought you might say that."

As they started walking, Calvin couldn't help but glance Lucy's way. Before his eyes, her icy persona had warmed to true friendliness—especially when she was talking to his chatty, outspoken sister.

He felt like she was even beginning to let down her guard around him. Was she finally warming up to him? He wondered again why she was so skittish from the start. Was she simply shy around men—or had another man hurt her badly?

That was something he intended to find out.

Chapter 6

"Oh, Mattie. I'm afraid I have terrible news," her mother said when she arrived at Mattie's side in the waiting room.

Mattie looked at her mother in confusion. Soon after they'd arrived at the center, Mattie had been taken to the back to get blood drawn and her vitals checked.

Because such things always took a long time, her mother had left, promising to return with some coffee and a bottle of water in an hour or so. Now she was waiting to meet with the doctor.

"What happened?" Mattie asked. Gripping the sides of the chair, she prepared herself for the worst. "Did you see the *doktah*? Did he tell you more test results?"

A chill went through her. Oh dear God. What if they already had discovered that all the cancer wasn't gone? What if she was going to have to have more surgery?

Or . . . what if things were even worse than that?

A flash of awareness and guilt entered her mother's eyes. "Oh! Oh, no, dear. It is bad news, but it has nothing to do with your doctor visit. I'm sorry if I scared you."

"If it's not that, what is it?"

Her mother took a chair. "The news is from Charlie. I asked if he could use his cell phone to check the messages on the phone line we share with the neighbors. He did, and then just came to tell me that we received a message from Lucy."

The momentary relief she'd felt fled in a heartbeat. "From Lucy? What happened? Is their train delayed?"

"Lucy's train broke down in Toledo."

"Oh my goodness! Is she okay?"

"She gave no indication that she was not. However, her next train doesn't leave until five o'clock this afternoon. Her train won't pull into Cleveland until after seven this evening. "

"Poor Lucy." Thinking about her pretty cousin, and her shy, reserved nature, Mattie shook her head. "What is she going to do today? And what about when she gets to Cleveland?"

Her mother crossed her legs. "That, at least, is something we won't have to worry about. I spoke to Charlie, and he said he would drive to Cleveland and meet her there."

"That is kind of him."

"I agree. We have much to be thankful for."

"I wonder what went wrong with the train."

"I guess we'll find out when we see her. All Lucy said

was that she wouldn't arrive on time, but for us not to worry."

"That was sweet of her to say, but I'll still worry." As she thought about all that Lucy was doing for her, traveling by herself, promising to help her through chemotherapy for a whole month, Mattie felt guiltier than ever. "She is still a fragile sort, Mamm."

"I know that."

"She doesn't trust much." Guilt slammed her hard. "Maybe she should have never come this way. Maybe I shouldn't have asked her to."

"You forget that this was Lucy's offer, not your request," her mother reminded her. "I'm sure she wouldn't have made the offer if she hadn't been sincere in heart."

She might have sincerely wanted to help, but a journey like the one she was having could lead to a lot of regrets. "Perhaps."

"Of course this is true." Patting her hand against the table, her mother struggled to her feet. "Don't you forget, that our Lord God is guiding our every move. He knows what is best for us. Never doubt that."

A true, sweet smile smoothed her brow. "Now, as soon as you meet with the doctor, we'll be on our way. And I intend to definitely ask Charlie if he'd please stop at Bob Evans on the way home. I'm hungry for more than ice cream. The women won't expect us until after lunchtime."

In spite of the nagging irritation she felt from her mother's insistence that she join the group, Mattie's mouth watered. "Do you think he'd mind going to the restaurant?"

"Not if he has time . . . and we offer to buy him his meal," she said with a wink.

The door opened and a nurse stepped out. "Mattie, are you ready?"

Mattie stood up. "I am. I'll be back soon, Mamm."

"Don't worry about me, dear. I'll have plenty to do, as always."

Mattie smiled weakly as her mother's words rested in the air. She knew what her mother meant. She was going to spend the time praying while Mattie was with the doctor.

Praying, like she always did.

At one time, Mattie had believed that prayer did help. That prayers were answered. She'd believed that with all her heart.

Now, though, she knew differently.

Because if God had been guiding her every move, then for some reason He had decided that she needed to have cancer. If God had been with her, He wanted her to have a terrible scar. And to be having chemotherapy.

And if He wanted her to experience all of that, she wished He would tell her why.

She really had no idea what she had done to deserve it.

The last time Lucy had shared a meal in a restaurant with a man, it had been with Paul. They had gone to town on a Saturday morning. And because the weather was bright and sunny, Paul had suggested they eat at a nearby restaurant that had an outside patio. Of course, she hadn't refused his offer. Her husband's word had always been final.

Much of their time during the meal was spent in silence. Paul had been more interested in the other people dining around them. Often, he'd stood up and left. She'd sat alone and tried not to look like she minded, sitting there by herself.

After all, she'd known better than to behave any differently.

Now, as she walked next to Katie and Calvin on the sidewalk outside the train station, Lucy couldn't help but think of how different the situation was. Katie, with her chatter and smiles, was making what would have been an awkward situation seem almost fun.

But it wasn't Katie who Lucy kept thinking about.

Whenever she looked Calvin's way or heard his voice, a tingly sort of awareness would appear inside her. She'd been always aware of Paul, too. But instead of stemming from fear, these new feelings were from the pleasure of Calvin's company. It was as if her body knew exactly where he was and responded with breathlessness. He was so handsome, sturdy. Bigger than Paul. More muscular, too, but also a bit like a teddy bear. Paul's body was wiry, like a fox.

Calvin exuded confidence. On the outside, he seemed as sure of himself as Paul had been. But Lucy was beginning to see that Calvin's self-confidence wasn't a wall to hide behind. No, it seemed to burn brightly from inside of him.

He was patient even while his eyes were curious and searching. He'd ask questions and was interested in her answers—and because of this Calvin didn't feel overpowering to her.

Instead of chiding her for walking too slowly, as Paul always had, Calvin didn't seem to mind waiting for her. Instead of getting mad at her for forgetting her quilt bag, he'd tried to help.

And now, when she stumbled next to him, he didn't act as if the little misstep was a reflection on him. Instead, he held out an arm to catch her. To help her steady herself. It was all terribly courteous.

Though she had no need for another man in her life, her emotions and heart told a different story. After a year living as a widow, her senses were once again attuned to a man's. But instead of feeling fear and worry when she looked at him, Lucy felt mesmerized.

"Ladies, you can order anything you'd like. My treat," Calvin said when they'd received their menus at the diner.

"Yours and the train company's," Lucy corrected with a grin. "We each got a meal voucher."

While he smiled right back, Katie started pointing to pictures on the menu. "What does all this say, Calvin?"

"It says you can have whatever you want, whenever you want it." Patiently, he pointed to a picture of pancakes. "See? They serve pancakes all day here."

"I wish we did that at home," Katie said. "I like pancakes all the time."

After they ordered, and Lucy was enjoying her hot coffee, Calvin leaned forward. "You know what? It just occurred to me that I never asked *why* you were traveling to Cleveland. You're not stopping in the city, are you?"

"Oh, no. I'm headed to a small town near Middlefield."

"We are as well. Where, exactly, are you going?"

"Jacob's Crossing."

Calvin looked truly taken aback. So stunned, Lucy looked at him curiously. "Have you heard of it? It's not very big."

"I should say we definitely have heard of Jacob's Crossing. That's where we live." Beside him, Katie giggled.

"Truly?" She'd never heard of such a coincidence.

"Truly." He grinned. "Who are you intending to see?"

She cleared her throat. "My cousin Mattie. Mattie Lapp."

His bark of laughter startled her. "The Lapp's farm is adjacent to ours. We're practically neighbors."

Lucy shook her head in wonder as the waitress delivered their plates of food. What were the chances that two strangers seated next to each other on a train would just happen to be going to the same place?

There was only one thing to credit their meeting to. Obviously the Lord had His hand on this situation. For some reason, He had intended that the two of them meet.

After joining him and Katie in a silent prayer, Lucy picked up her fork and stabbed a piece of sausage.

When they were almost done, Calvin sipped his coffee and picked up their earlier conversation. "Lucy, are you visiting Mattie because of her sickness?"

"I am. She's been in a mighty bad way, you know."

"Indeed, she has. We've all been worried about her. Not only do our lands border each other, but we've been friends of a sort all our lives. My brother Graham is especially close to her. He's taken her diagnosis terribly hard, I'm afraid."

Lucy looked at him curiously. "I didn't know she had a sweetheart."

"They're not close in that way. Just close as friends."

She couldn't imagine being friends with a man. "Oh."

After the waitress took away their plates and poured Calvin more coffee, he gazed out the window. "She, uh, has just had surgery."

"It was a difficult operation for her, I fear."

"Her mother said the same thing."

"I am going to be staying with her for a month. To help her recover and to be with her during her chemotherapy treatments."

"I'm sure she is thankful for you."

"No more than I am thankful for her." It was hard not to think of Mattie without remembering how strong she'd been when Lucy had been recovering from Paul's death. "We've been through a lot together."

"Even though you live in Michigan and she lives in Ohio?"

"Yes. She's, uh, come to visit me several times. To be honest, I haven't been out to Jacob's Crossing in years. I'm anxious to see it again."

"Don't be too anxious. Not much ever changes there."

He sounded so aggrieved, she chuckled. "Believe me, I'm counting on that. I like things to stay the same." Then, recalling how many changes she'd been through, she amended her words. "I mean, I like most things to stay the same. The good things."

Though Calvin looked at her curiously, he didn't say anything.

Later, after they'd finished and had exited the diner, Calvin looked up at the fancy clock tower across the street from them. "It's only twelve-thirty."

"We are going to have a terribly long day."

"I have an idea," Calvin blurted. "On the train, I read a magazine article about the Toledo Zoo. It's supposed to be a mighty nice zoo. Would you ladies care to go?"

Katie's eyes widened. "Oh, Calvin, can we?"

"I don't see why not. We've got hours."

Katie grabbed Lucy's hand. "Please say yes."

Calvin's eyes shone. "You really should. It will be fun. I promise, I won't let anything happen to you. You'll be safe with me."

Though protective instincts were calling out to her not to trust him, Lucy found herself ignoring the warning voices. She wanted to do something fun. "All right," she said. "I will be happy to join you all."

Katie squeezed Lucy's hand and smiled, and Calvin nodded. *"Gut!"*

"What about your uncle? Should we go see if he wants to join us?"

Calvin shook his head. "He did say earlier that he wanted to sit and relax. Wandering around a zoo would be the opposite of that. No, it will just be the three of us."

He looked so pleased, Lucy felt her cheeks heat—at first with pleasure, because she made him happy, then with embarrassment. Here she was, twenty-four years old, and this man was making her feel like a schoolgirl!

But certainly it was past time she had an adventure or two. Later, when they were back on the train, she'd have plenty of time to worry about what she was getting herself into.

"Do you know how to call a taxi?" she asked.

"I've never done it, but it shouldn't be too hard," he said, scanning the near-empty street. "If we ever see one drive by," he added, his voice dry.

Because the road did appear empty, and her heart felt so light, she teased him back: "Finding a taxicab should be only as difficult as it would be to find a horse and buggy."

"Or, for us, a train that worked," he murmured.

Unable to help herself, she tilted her head back and laughed.

And felt even lighter when Calvin joined in.

Chapter 7

"Mattie, isn't this such a wonderful-*gut* activity? I knew as soon as we got around our friends, our spirits would lift."

Mattie smiled and nodded from her chair at the edge of the Knepps' kitchen. Privately, however, she wished she was sitting almost anywhere else. It was hard to watch ladies and girls her age bustle around the kitchen . . . making fried pies to sell. For her benefit.

When her mother gave her a meaningful look, Mattie cleared her throat. "Yes. I mean, I'm terribly grateful for you all."

"Don't think anything of it," Gwen Kent said as she cut more shortening into the dough. "It's a pleasure."

"Well, all I know is that these will be the flakiest fried pies anyone has ever tasted, for sure," her mother said. "People will snap them up."

"Oh, they will," Joanne Knepp said confidently. "Everyone likes a *gut* fried pie, for a wonderful cause."

Gwen darted another smile her way.

"The way you all are working so hard in our makeshift assembly line practically brings tears to my eyes," Mattie's mom said to everyone.

Mrs. Knepp chuckled. "We work so well together, we're almost professional, *jah?*"

Feeling left out, Mattie got to her feet. "Maybe I could help box them up?"

Mrs. Kent waved away her offer with one hand. "Oh, please don't, dear. I'd feel awful if you wore yourself out. All you need to do is get better soon."

"I agree," Mrs. Knepp said. "It's enough that you're here. And making these pies gives me a nice reason to enjoy everyone's company. All I've been doing is either spring cleaning or working in the garden."

"*Jah.* Having an excuse to be in the company of other women all day is a wonderful-*gut* thing," Mrs. Lapp agreed. "Mattie, are you comfortable?"

"Mighty comfortable. *Danke.*" Mrs. Knepp had pulled into the kitchen one of the upholstered chairs from her front room.

After carefully taking two pies out of hot oil and setting them on an old newspaper to dry, Mrs. Knepp said, "Mattie, you had a doctor's appointment today, yes?"

Pure dismay coursed through her as she realized that all the women in the room had just perked right up. "*Jah,*" she said.

"Did you learn any news?"

Mattie felt her stomach sting. "It was just a checkup."

Her mother jumped into the conversation. "Mattie's stitches are healing nicely, though he was a bit concerned about some of her blood work. He asked you to rest as much as possible." She nodded. "Right, Mattie?"

What could she say? Weakly, Mattie nodded—though an evil part of her wanted to glare at her mother. Really, if she was that concerned about her welfare, shouldn't she have taken her home—instead of putting her on display in someone's kitchen?

After the women made some clucking noises, Mrs. Knepp asked, "Mattie, won't your cousin be here soon to help?"

"Lucy will be here this evening."

"She'll have to come over. I'll introduce her to lots of people," Gwen said.

Just as if Lucy was coming out to vacation.

Mattie fought to keep a smile on her face. Honestly, it felt like no one really understood how weak she felt. How dismayed. How worried she was about her future.

Her mother spoke. "Unfortunately, Lucy's train broke down in Toledo, and she has to spend most of her day there."

"Poor Lucy," Mrs. Knepp said. "I remember meeting her years ago. I would have hoped her journey was easier."

"I would have hoped so, too, but one must deal with what one is given," her mother said with a meaningful look Mattie's way. "I have faith that she'll get through this challenge well and good, and have a story to tell."

"At least one," Mattie said drily.

Mrs. Knepp's eyes twinkled. "In any case, Lucy's arrival should cheer you up, Mattie dear. And that is the most important thing, yes? And I bet a few of these wonderful-*gut* pies will, too."

"I like the lemon ones," Hannah Kent said.

"Me too, dear," Mrs. Kent said with a smile. Wiping her hands on her apron, she continued: "Now, let's finish up this task so Ella can sell them at the market on Saturday."

"I wish I could go and sell them, too," Hannah whispered.

"Ella will see that not a one is left over," her mother assured her. "Ella Hostetler is such a serious young woman. Always thinking about others."

"Do you think we'll ever sell pies again?" Hannah asked.

"I'm afraid so," Mrs. Kent said with a grimace. "Treating cancer is an expensive undertaking."

Her eyes full of compassion, Mrs. Knepp walked over and gently clasped Mattie's shoulder. "We'll do whatever it takes to help with the costs. Everyone here in Jacob's Crossing will."

"I appreciate that," said Mattie's mother gently.

And as the room quieted, Mattie felt her depression grab on to her more tightly. Not only was she terribly sick, but the illness was putting an awful burden on her family.

"Gwen, cheer us all up," Mrs. Knepp said brightly. "Tell us what is going on between you and Will Kauffman."

Gwen sighed, her green eyes turning dreamy. "Oh, nothing much. We are merely seeing each other."

"Seeing each other seriously," Gwen's mother corrected with a smile.

Mrs. Knepp clapped her hands. "Gwen, should we be talking about wedding suppers yet?"

"Not at all," Gwen replied, a pretty blush staining her cheeks. "Will and I are simply spending time together."

As the women started discussing Will and Gwen, and a few other new couples in their community, Mattie closed her eyes and pretended to fall asleep.

It was too hard to sit and smile . . . realizing that she might never be like Gwen.

If the chemotherapy didn't work, or her cancer came back . . . she would never be thinking about a man of her own.

John didn't regret passing on the walk with Calvin, Lucy, and Katie in the slightest. Though he loved their company, it had been a long while since he'd spent so much time in the constant company of others. A little privacy was no problem.

And, for that matter, he didn't necessarily think Calvin and Lucy were going to miss his presence all that much anyway. There was something going on between them— he was certain of that.

Even if they both seemed to be oblivious to those sparks.

After getting a cold drink, he found a quiet table and opened up his laptop. In no time, he was surfing the web, reading e-mails, and catching up on Facebook. As he read different posts, he replied to a few, clicked "like" for a couple others.

And then he spied Angela's picture.

His ex-wife. He hadn't heard from her in years, hadn't

thought about her in years. And now, not only had he been thinking about her on the train, but here she was, posting about a new puppy she was training to be a guide dog.

John's fingers hovered over the keys. Every nerve inside him screamed to ignore her profile picture. To not revisit his past.

But, unable to resist the temptation of seeing her again, he clicked on the photo anyway.

Her dark eyes staring back at him brought forth another rush of memories. Oh, why did she still have to be so pretty? Like a starving man, he scanned her profile information. Noticed that she was married. Had two children.

Obviously nothing ever stayed the same.

He remembered their many arguments about their future. Time and again, she'd pushed off his talk about having a baby one day. All she'd ever wanted was a pretty house and the freedom to shop and do as she pleased—without her family's suffocating closeness.

Though he hadn't understood her need to distance herself from her parents, especially when they'd helped him so much, John had ached to make her happy. So, he'd never said a word when she insisted they stop visiting her family for Sunday dinner.

When she'd teased him about his *Amish* ways, he worked even harder to fit into the English world. He stopped talking about things that were important to him and worked hard. He'd bought her the things she said she wanted.

But, eventually, those things had not been enough.

And then his lack of education hadn't been enough.

And then, one day, she'd told him that he hadn't been enough.

All of a sudden, the pain of her rejection stung him as if it had just happened. Not years ago. Feeling frustrated with himself, he quickly shut down his computer and put it away.

He should have known better. It was hard enough to go back to Jacob's Crossing—the last thing he needed was to spend more time on his failings with Angela, too.

After fishing out his book, he gave all his attention to the mystery. Yes, it was far better to concentrate on this story than his past. Or his future.

Or on how sometimes he felt sure Angela had been exactly right—he wasn't enough, and he never would be.

Chapter 8

"Mattie, are you all right?" her mother asked through the bathroom door. "You've been in there quite some time."

Struggling for patience, Mattie replied, "I'm fine. I just wanted to get cleaned up."

"Oh. Well, yes. I suppose it was a *verra* long day. Do you need help getting dressed?"

"*Nee.* I can still dress myself, Mamm," she said sharply. More sharply than she had intended.

"I know you can. I just thought you might need—"

"I don't." Mattie could hear her mother's feet shuffling a bit, like she was trying to walk away from the other side of the door but couldn't.

"Oh. All right, then. I will go work on the laundry . . . if you need me—" She paused. "Do, uh, you need some of your laundry done?"

It took almost all the energy she had not to snap at her mother. Not to tell her to give her some space.

But that wouldn't be right, of course. Here her mother was trying so hard. Trying so hard to be helpful and positive—showing her love through her perpetual busyness. Mattie knew from experience that being happy and strong for someone else was difficult to do.

"I don't need anything washed," she finally said, "but thank you. I'll be out soon," Mattie promised. As soon as she heard her mother step away, she sighed. Oh, but she needed to free herself from this anger that seemed to have taken hold of her and didn't want to let go.

It gripped her when she was least aware of it and pulled her unapologetically into a dark depression. Worse, she never knew what would set her off.

Today, it had been the extra blood tests that the doctor had ordered. Although he said it was a normal occurrence, Mattie just wasn't sure. Always in the back of her mind, there was a dark thread of awareness brewing. There was always a chance that the cancer could return.

Those worries had stewed and grown when they'd been at the Knepps'.

She felt weighed down. All she saw when she looked in the mirror was a girl who was less than she used to be, who was damaged before she even had a chance at life.

Turning away, Mattie quickly fastened her dress together, then left the bathroom. She felt the cooler air of the hall fan her face as she walked to the kitchen. She listened for her mother's voice as she approached.

But the voice that greeted her was far deeper. "Mattie, I

was wondering when you were going to appear. It's about time, I think."

"Daed! I didn't know you were home."

He shrugged as he stood awkwardly facing her, his hands behind his back. "I thought I might do some things around the house today. It's been a while since I weeded the flower beds."

Mattie couldn't remember her father *ever* weeding the beds. But perhaps this was just her father's way of spending more time with her?

She stepped forward and took his arm. "It's *gut* you're home when it's daylight."

He laughed. "I am enjoying it as well, though I feel a little out of sorts, if you want to know the truth."

"That's because you're used to spending every day with the dairy cows."

"Most likely. However, I'm hoping that perhaps the cows can do without me for a time."

"I'm sure they'll do their best, though they might make you pay for your neglect tomorrow," she teased. For as long as she could remember, her father had always said the cows had a jealous streak a mile long.

"Their jealousy might be bearable if you will spend some time with me this afternoon, daughter."

"Of course I will. What would you like to do?"

"Would you like to sit outside for a bit while I tend the flowers?"

"I could help you—"

"No, you could not. You may not weed, daughter."

She'd always hated weeding. She hated how it was a

constant thing, and how more often than not the weeds never failed to have prickers that bit into her hands.

How ironic that now that she couldn't pull dandelions, she ached to do so. Anything to give her a sense of normalcy. "I'll try to only watch."

He quirked an eyebrow. "Try?"

"All right. I promise I will not weed. I'll just sit and watch you work."

"Then, you may join me."

She sat in the shade and watched him work, liking how his beard was so light it blended with his tan skin. Her dad was such a good man. A kind man, to both her and her mother. Hopefully one day she would find a man so wonderful. *If* she would survive to be a wife and mother.

Ah, the darkness had come again. "Daed, do you think I'll ever get better?" she blurted.

Abruptly, he stilled. "Well . . . I hope so. I hope and pray that you will. That's all we can do, *jah?*"

She nodded. Because he hadn't been overly optimistic, she felt comforted. For some reason hearing his words, so plainspoken and bare, gave her more of a sense of peace than all the flowery promises her mother constantly spouted.

And for the first time since the doctor had calmly told her she had cancer, Mattie felt a little ray of sun filter through her cloud of depression.

Maybe she was going to be okay after all.

Having cancer wasn't easy. But living without hope was even harder.

* * *

Lucy knew she'd never forget their day at the Toledo Zoo. After arriving there in the taxi, she, Katie, and Calvin explored the grounds as much as their time had allowed.

Katie had laughed at the hippos and Calvin had enjoyed the monkeys. She was interested in all of the beautiful historic buildings that made up the zoo, and enthralled about the idea of the men of the Great Depression building such things of beauty.

It had reminded her that it was always best to move forward, instead of dwelling on the past.

But even more special than the architecture and the antics of the animals were her companions. Lucy had truly loved her time with Katie and Calvin Weaver.

Katie, with her spunk and mischievous ways, reminded Lucy of her little brothers and sisters.

And Calvin . . . his way of looking at the world, with joy and amusement in almost everything, made her happy.

For the first time in months, she felt a true sense of optimism. A true feeling of hope for her future. Perhaps one day she really would be able to live without fear, without anxiety. Maybe this trip to Ohio was the fresh start she'd been needing.

As they crossed the street, Lucy pointed out a horse and buggy. "Our buggies would feel very different if they looked like that, wouldn't they?" Lucy teased.

"My *mamm* wouldn't like it none," Katie declared. "It's too . . . too everything."

"You said that exactly right, Katie," Calvin said. "It is *too* everything, indeed."

The buggy was a tourist attraction, to be sure, as fancy

as anything she'd ever seen—with ribbons and bands of flowers adorning a painted carriage. A young couple was standing next to the horse and getting their picture taken.

Calvin followed her gaze and pointed. "Look at how that driver has it all decorated. It's nearly blinding. Beauty wouldn't care for all those decorations on his harness."

Katie giggled. "Oh, no, he wouldn't!"

Lucy was grinning, too, when she felt Calvin tense. "Katie, you stay with Lucy. I'll be right back," he muttered before striding up the block. Right to where the carriage was parked.

Katie tightened her grip on Lucy's hand. "What's he doing?"

"I'm not sure," Lucy murmured. She almost ignored his directive and followed, but then stood frozen in shock as she watched him loosen the horse's lines and direct people away from it.

When a man who was obviously the horse and buggy's owner started yelling at Calvin, he stood his ground.

Beside her, Katie murmured, "Oh, my. Look how mad Calvin is at the driver!"

"He's mad?"

"Uh-huh. Calvin never yells, he just scowls, like he's doing now."

Lucy swallowed the lump that had just formed in her throat. "Your brother certainly is scowling. I wonder why he doesn't just walk away? It's not his horse."

Looking up at her, Katie shook her head. "My brother would never do that. Not if he was upset, anyways. Calvin doesn't back down."

With a sinking feeling, Lucy watched the driver fold his arms over his chest and yell. Though Calvin didn't seem to be yelling, too, Lucy noticed that he didn't back off one bit.

Actually, Calvin looked to be terribly angry. Every so often, he would point at the horse and glare. When a young couple approached, obviously eager for a carriage ride, instead of moving to one side, Calvin shook his head.

The driver's voice rose as the couple scurried away.

As she watched all of this unfold, Lucy's insides turned to ice. Was this the real man she was seeing? The real Calvin underneath all the jokes and kidding? A man who could let anger overcome him, reducing everyone around to silence?

Lucy blinked as the driver said something and turned away. Then practically dropped her jaw when Calvin stepped forward and argued again.

Even from her distance, Lucy saw that Calvin was in the man's space. Standing so close that the man had no choice but to listen. Just like Paul used to do to her.

Though Calvin wasn't touching the man, Lucy recalled Paul gripping her shoulder, his fingers digging into the soft muscles of her shoulder.

Calvin wasn't actually yelling at the driver, but Lucy could almost hear Paul yelling at her. Saying such awful things that her ears would ring.

"Lucy, your hand's all clammy."

"Sorry." Pulling her hand away, she wiped her palm on the skirt of her dress, then placed both hands protectively on Katie's shoulders.

Tears pricked her eyes as she pushed the awful memories away. Forced herself to look toward Calvin, hoping that he had turned back into the calm, patient, fun-filled man she'd gotten to know that day. The man she'd started to believe in.

But that man had vanished, right before her eyes.

Calvin's voice became more harsh. Lucy noticed his hands were balled into fists at his sides. Then, when the man started to walk away, Calvin grabbed his shoulder.

Against her will, she flinched. "Oh, this is terrible," she murmured.

When she gripped her apron with both hands, Katie used the freedom to rush forward.

"Katie? Katie, come back!" Lucy called out.

"I'll be fine. Calvin needs me," she said as she weaved her way through the people, then stopped at his side.

Lucy held her breath, half waiting for Calvin to turn on his sister. But he didn't. Instead, he took her hand in his and kept talking.

But Lucy had seen enough.

Unable to stand there another minute, she crossed to the opposite corner of the intersection and scurried down the sidewalk, taking care to keep her head down and to look away from the small crowd around Calvin.

Picking up her pace, she practically raced the last two blocks to the train terminal and burst through the doors. A few people looked up at her arrival, but then turned away.

Thankful for some peace at last, she slowly walked to the electronic board showing the train schedule. Noticing that her train was still due to leave at five, Lucy looked for the quietest, most out-of-the-way spot that she could find.

She would sit there and wait. Wait for the train to come, so she could board and get to Cleveland. And while she waited, she made a vow right then and there to never think the best of Calvin Weaver ever again. She had seen his true colors.

Chapter 9

"You did the best you could," a man nearby told Calvin as he and Katie were about to walk away from the horrible driver and his rig.

"Not enough, obviously," Calvin replied, filled with regret. When Katie sidled up closer to him, he reached out and gently rubbed her arm. "Tomorrow, that poor horse will be walking the same streets, in pain."

"Maybe, or maybe not. A lot of people around us heard what you had to say," the man said thoughtfully. "A couple of people even told me they were going to make some calls to the animal welfare league."

"I'll pray that something gets done, then. I feel bad for losin' my temper, but I hate to see any animal getting abused. It ain't right. That poor mare's knee was terribly swollen." He swallowed hard.

"She was near starving, too."

"That driver didn't even look like he cared. All he seemed worried about was if he could drive that poor horse another four hours." The waste of such a fine animal made his heart sink.

"Something will get done, sooner or later. We'll all make some calls, and who knows—maybe that guy heard you after all and will get the horse some treatment."

"I can only pray that he did," Calvin said fervently.

After another awkward look of sympathy, the man left, leaving Calvin alone with Katie. Bending so they were eye level, he searched his little sister's gaze. "I hope I didn't scare you. It's just that, well, I felt terribly sorry for that horse."

"I felt badly for it, too," Katie whispered. "We're much nicer to Beauty."

Pressing his lips to her brow, he smiled. "You're right. Compared to that mare, our Beauty is a right lucky horse." Straightening, he held out his hand. "Well, the best thing to do now is get Lucy and catch our train."

"I canna wait to go home," Katie replied, then stopped. "But I don't see Lucy."

With dismay, Calvin looked for Lucy, too.

What if something had happened to her! It would be all his fault. He should have minded his responsibilities better, instead of caring so much about something he couldn't change. "Lucy?" he called out again as he walked back to the spot where he'd left them.

"Katie, where do you think she went? Did you see her go?"

A wrinkle formed between Katie's brows. "I thought she was gonna stay nearby. But maybe she went back to the train station?"

"I guess she could have." After all, she certainly wasn't anywhere they could see. "Hmm. I wonder why she would have left . . ."

"I don't know. But she looked upset."

"We better go find her." Though he knew it didn't make a lot of sense, Calvin felt a bit put out. If she suddenly didn't want to wait for him, the least she could have done was walk Katie to his side. Katie was just a little girl. After all, all day long they'd been by each other's sides, enjoying each other's company.

"Calvin?" she asked hesitantly, looking up at him. "Did you fix the horse?"

"*Nee.*"

"The man looked mad at you."

"That's okay. I was mad at him, too."

"Do you think Mamm would've gotten mad at you for talking to the man? She says we're supposed to be kind to everyone."

Calvin thought about that. "She might have gotten mad at me. And I should have probably kept to myself, but that poor mare needed some help." He shrugged. "Sometimes, a man has to do what he feels is right, even if it might be wrong." Realizing how confusing he just sounded, he looked down at his sister. "Did I make any sense to you?"

"*Nee.*"

Calvin chuckled. "I was afraid of that. Well, don't worry none. We'll find Lucy and then get on the train."

They held hands the rest of the way to the terminal, and finally found Lucy twenty minutes later. She was sitting in a corner, reading a home-and-garden magazine. Immediately, the muscles in his shoulders relaxed. He'd begun to really worry about her safety.

"I've been lookin' for you all over," Calvin said. "Why did you run off?"

After briefly smiling at Katie, Lucy turned to him, her eyes flat, nearly void of all expression. "You were otherwise occupied."

What in the world? He swallowed. "I was talking to that man about his mare. You know that."

The muscles in her jaw tightened. "That's not all you were doing. You were yelling at him."

"I was, but it didn't help, I don't think," he said with a shake of his head. "That man didn't look like he was of a mind to listen to me at all."

"I . . . I didn't know you had a temper, Calvin. I didn't know you were like that."

"Like what?" He was completely bewildered—and taken aback by *her* anger. "Lucy, did you see that poor horse?"

"Yes, but she wasn't who I was concerned with. I was looking at you."

"Well, you should have spared a moment for that poor animal," he retorted. "She was in a mighty bad way. You could nearly count her ribs! And I think her knee has an infection. She needs a course of antibiotics and a few weeks off. He's going to kill her, making her work like that . . ." His voice slowed when he realized she wasn't listening.

Instead, she seemed to be looking beyond him, at something that wasn't quite there. "You grabbed his shoulder."

Calvin remembered that well. "I know I did. He turned away when I was trying to show him the swell—Lucy, what is wrong?"

"Everything." With measured movements, Lucy closed the magazine and set it neatly next to her. "I'm sorry to say this, but . . . I have no desire to be in your company again."

"What?" Surely he wasn't hearing her right. "Lucy, what did I do that got you so upset?"

"Before . . . before I saw you yell . . . I had thought that maybe you were different. I mean . . . you seemed like such a calm person." Her eyes softened as she turned to his sister. "Katie, this has nothing to do with you. I've truly enjoyed getting to know you. Perhaps our paths will cross in Jacob's Crossing."

Biting her lip, Katie simply nodded.

But it wasn't in Calvin's mind-set to give up so easily. "Lucy, you're not making sense."

"I'm sorry you feel that way."

Irritation sliced through him. "And once more, I *am* a calm person." When she merely raised her brows, he amended his words. "Well, all right. I guess I do sometimes let my temper get the best of me. Sometimes I just can't help myself. But I am working on it. The Lord knows I try my best."

"You couldn't help yourself," she echoed.

His shirt collar was getting tight. "That's right. It's a fault of mine," he said, struggling to find a way to tell Lucy about how he just couldn't abide to see animals abused.

How something inside of him just snapped, and he'd known he had to at least try to make things better.

Just like he was doing now.

But instead of looking like she wanted to hear what he had to say, she scooted a bit farther away from him. "I see."

"No, you don't. Lucy, that man's *gall* . . . that horse, well . . . Someone needed to take its side, *jah*?"

But instead of warming to him, or talking about how she, too, had felt sorry for the horse, Lucy picked up her magazine and flipped it open.

Leaving him dumbfounded. "Are you going to ignore me now?" Feeling Katie's unease, he wrapped his arm around her shoulders. "You're going to ignore us both?"

The magazine snapped shut. "Calvin, please. Please just give me some space."

Though her expression was pleading . . . though he heard almost a desperation in her voice, Calvin didn't feel he could do that. "But we just spent the day together," he protested. "We had popcorn, and walked and walked . . ." And he was remembering the way she had smiled at him . . . remembering the way she'd laughed by his side, and struggled to come to terms with what she was saying. "Lucy, I thought you enjoyed yourself."

"I did. It was *wunderbaar*." A flash of pain entered her golden eyes before she blinked and it went away. "But our day is over now."

Over. He stepped back. It seemed as if Lucy had just decided to reject him because he dared to defend an animal. Rejecting him just as Gwen had done when she'd gotten tired of waiting for him to propose to her.

Hurt and confusion flowed through him like a raging river.

But he was still enough of a man to know that he didn't need this. "All right. I trust that you will get on the train just fine without my assistance?"

"I got on it just fine without you, Calvin. I'm sure I will be able to board again, too."

"Then I'll leave you." Looking at Katie, he added grimly, "We'll leave you in peace."

"Katie, I am sorry," Lucy murmured.

Bending down to his sister, Calvin said, "Let's find something else to do." Then he took her hand and walked away. As the space between him and Lucy grew, Calvin found himself waiting for her to call out to him. To tell him she was sorry. To tell him to come back and explain things better.

But instead, all he heard was Lucy flip a page of her magazine. As if he, and his sister, hardly mattered to her at all.

Chapter 10

"What is this?" Paul asked, holding up her diary.

He'd found it! Unable to speak, she stared at him from the doorway of their bedroom. Afraid to come any closer.

To her dismay, he bent down and picked up more note-books. All her journals from the last five years. "Why did you write such things?" he asked, opening one and holding it up to her.

Even from her distance, she saw it was a very old diary. The curlicued handwriting showed that she'd written the entry when she was probably no more than seventeen.

Oh, what had consumed her then? Lucy couldn't even re-member.

A glimmer of hope filled her. Perhaps that was the only journal he'd read?

"It's just a habit," she finally said. "I— It's nothing for you to worry about."

"Everything you do concerns me," Paul said, crossing the room. Walking to her. "You will burn these."

She nodded. Almost grateful that was the worst that had happened. So grateful that he hadn't read her thoughts about him. About how she wished he'd leave her. Leave her alone.

Lucy's eyes popped open.

Ah, she'd been dreaming again. She shook her head, attempting to clear it. Oh, but that would have been a terrible thing, if Paul had ever found her diaries.

But he never had.

She forced herself to dwell on what Paul's reaction to her missing journal would have been. Because, surely, there could be nothing worse than that.

Whoever had found her journal had most likely thrown it away.

Her words would never be found. Never read.

And no one else would ever know just how glad she was that her husband was dead.

By his estimation, they had little more than an hour left of their journey.

Calvin was bored. Katie had fallen asleep, John was busy playing solitaire on his laptop computer, and Lucy, of course, was somewhere down the aisle.

Ignoring him.

Restless, he opened his backpack, searching for the newspaper. Then he noticed the book he'd picked up when it had slid down the aisle. He pulled it out and ran his hand across the leather binding.

Lucy's journal.

The right thing to do would be to get up and go take it to her. But there was no doubt in his mind that she'd say he stole it, or some other such nonsense.

The book, with its tan leather cover, was a heavy thing. Suddenly, he was curious about Lucy's handwriting. Was it as prim and proper as the rest of her?

Somehow he was sure it would be. No doubt every letter would be painstakingly formed. She probably recorded each day's weather and documented every minuscule event.

Giving in to temptation, he opened the journal in the middle. Just to see what her handwriting looked like. The pages inside were slightly rough, as if they'd been written on front and back with a pencil.

To his surprise, the writing was far from a neat and tidy cursive. Instead of perfectly formed letters, he found lazily sprawled sentences, some words running into the next, like she wrote in a hurry.

Or perhaps, without caring.

A flicker of unease went through him. He should close the cover immediately and walk it down the aisle to Lucy. The contents were definitely none of his business. What she wrote was personal.

He would be invading her privacy in the very worst way.

But still he looked.

I'm glad he's dead. I don't miss him. Sometimes—and I'm sorry, Lord—sometimes I wish he'd died sooner.

Stunned, Calvin slammed the book shut. Slipped the journal back in his backpack. Zipped it shut.

And closed his eyes, wishing he'd never picked up the journal.

But even with his eyes closed, Lucy's words seemed to be permanently etched in his brain. How could someone so sweet have so much evil and anger inside of her?

How could a woman he admired even think such a sin?

It was troubling, indeed.

Chapter 11

One by one, weary passengers exited the train. Following the rest of the crowd, Lucy stepped onto the moving stairs toward the main level of the terminal. The snack bar was closed, and only a few people stood in line at the ticket counters.

Lucy slumped a bit as she stared around her. For a brief instant, she'd been looking for Mattie's cheerful face. Aching for Mattie's usual bright smile of welcome. Mattie had always arrived in Michigan exuberantly—her arms wide open for a fierce hug.

But it was a wishful thought, of course. Lucy had come to Ohio to take care of Mattie, not be greeted by her.

Calvin, whom she had studiously been ignoring the whole time, squeezed through the crowd and approached. Right behind him was his shadow. Katie looked terribly cute and prim in her black bonnet. John was trailing behind them, talking on his cell phone.

Lucy stopped and waited for them to approach.

"I'm glad you stopped," Calvin said. "I thought I was going to have to chase you through the whole terminal."

Lucy supposed she deserved that. "I'm glad we will have the chance to say goodbye to each other." Lucy smiled at them both. "Well, I wish you well on the rest of your journey home."

His lips thinned. "Well, I see whatever was bothering you is still with you, alive and well."

"It's not likely to leave, Calvin. I know what I saw." Though a flicker of hurt flashed in his eyes, she pushed the slight feeling of guilt away.

She needed to remember just how kind Paul had been to her when they'd been courting. He'd been courteous and pleasant. And then, after she'd pledged to be his wife for life, he showed his true colors.

There was a good chance that Calvin was cut from the same cloth. And even if he wasn't, they would most likely never see each other again. They would soon part.

For that matter, she didn't need a man in her life at all. And most especially, not one with a temper.

Calvin adjusted the straps of his orange backpack as they continued the long walk to the baggage claim area. "How will you travel to Jacob's Crossing?"

"Charlie, Mattie's English driver, is going to pick me up at seven-thirty."

He looked at her worriedly. "That's quite a bit of time from now."

He was right. But it was how things went. "Not so much."

"Would you like us to wait with you?"

"Of course not." Though Lucy knew his concern for her was genuine, it felt confining all of a sudden. She didn't want to depend on him. "I'll stay inside, where there're lots of people," she said, taking care to keep her voice cool and collected. "Now, what about you?"

Calvin looked embarrassed. "My brothers are on their way."

"In a buggy?"

"Oh, no. They hired a driver." He flashed a smile. "I'm half surprised my Uncle John didn't want to rent a car, but perhaps this is just as easy for now."

Hearing about their plans made her feel empty. Even though she knew she was doing the right thing, it was still hard. "Well, I wish you well."

He gripped her shoulder just as she was turning away. "Lucy, stop—"

Her arm felt like it was on fire from his grip. With a shake, she pulled away from him. "*Nee*. We have . . . We have nothing else to say."

Stung, Calvin let his hand slowly fall to his side. "You don't think so? That is a shame."

His words were sharp. Painful to hear. For a split second, Lucy considered apologizing. Imagined grabbing his hand.

"Goodbye, Lucy."

"Goodbye. And . . . and thank you for taking me to the zoo. I liked it very much."

He frowned. "Perhaps I'll see you in Jacob's Crossing."

"Yes. I'm sure I'll see you there." Yes, no matter how much she might be tempted to give in, she needed to remind herself not to count on him. Not to forget how happy she'd once been with Paul. How he, too, had once pulled her in with an easy smile and shining eyes.

"All right, then," he said, but still, he looked unhappy. "Will you ever try to understand my point of view?"

"About the driver and the horse?"

He nodded.

She wanted to say she would. More than anything, she wanted to put all her fears behind her. But what would that mean?

Most likely that she hadn't learned a single thing from living with Paul.

She was tempted. A big part of her wanted to listen to him and believe him, and think he would never yell or get angry again.

But she'd already done that. Far too often, she'd listened to Paul's excuses. She'd believed his promises about changing. But of course, he never did.

She cleared her throat. "I know your temper just got the best of you."

A line formed between his brows. "Lucy, I promise, I'm not usually like that."

Paul had said that so often. That he hadn't meant to yell at her; that she just *made* him lose his temper. That he hadn't meant to break her arm. Or bruise her face. That she'd been so difficult.

And lazy.

Or ungrateful.

With effort, she tried to clear her head of the memories and move forward. "So . . . will both Loyal and Graham come for you?"

"I would be surprised if both didn't come. It's like them to do something like that, I think. One of us gets an idea, then the other two want a part in it. It used to drive my parents to distraction."

"I bet it did," Lucy said with a smile, in spite of her vow to stay aloof.

Before Calvin could reply, Katie interrupted. "I miss my brothers."

With relief, Lucy bent to face the little girl. "I'm sure you do," Lucy said. "And I'm sure they miss you!"

Katie tilted her head. "Will we see you in Jacob's Crossing?"

Looking Calvin's way again, she shrugged. "Perhaps."

"I hope so."

Calvin opened his mouth, then seemed to think the better of it and closed it again. Instead, he curved a hand around Katie's shoulder just as John approached.

"Best of luck to you, Lucy," John said.

"And you as well."

He grinned, rocking back on his heels. "Thank you. I'm going to need it. I have a feeling it's hard to start over again."

Beyond them, under the bright orange-yellow glow of the fluorescent lights, people were gathering and already pulling their bags off the cart. And Lucy knew she'd stalled long enough. It was time to go. Time to put this meeting, this chance relationship, back to where it was intended to be. In the past. "I best go get my suitcase and be on my way," she said. "And let you three get on your way as well—"

"Calvin! Katie!"

Lucy turned just in time to see two blond men engulf Calvin and Katie with warm hugs and hearty laughter, and shake John's hand with broad smiles.

With a lump in her throat, she tried not to stare. Tried not to notice just how much his brothers looked like Calvin. Tried not to see how his expression had changed, how it had become less guarded, almost more innocent-looking as they teased him and picked up Katie.

"I've got our girl," one of them said. "Graham, grab their bags and come on. The driver's charging us by the minute and mile."

"The drivers always do," Calvin said. Then, for a split second, he turned her way again.

And one more time, their eyes met. Lucy ached to say something, to say anything . . . anything to try to explain herself.

But then the baggage handler tossed another bag out into the area. Hers.

She hurriedly grabbed the handles.

"Not so fast, ma'am," the worker said. "You have to show your receipt."

"Oh, yes. Of course." Hurriedly, she pulled out the small slip of paper and handed it over. When she looked around again, the Weavers were gone.

She swallowed a lump in her throat and tried not to care.

* * *

"Calvin, you've been awfully quiet," Loyal said as they rode in the back of a van to Jacob's Crossing. "I would have thought you would have had more to say about your trip to Indiana."

Calvin glanced at his uncle, chatting with the driver in the front seat. "John, you want to add anything?"

He turned around and grinned at them, looking far younger than his thirty-eight years in the dim light. "Sorry, Calvin. I don't even want to think about our train trip right now. Feel free to tell Loyal and Graham all about it, though."

Loyal chuckled. "It was that good, hmm?"

Calvin grinned. "It was that bad. Actually, I probably would have had more to say if the adventure getting back here hadn't been quite so long," he said, trying to joke, but feeling like every word was getting stuck in his throat.

Graham leaned back in his seat. "Your journey does sound eventful, but still . . . you seem different somehow." He glanced toward Katie, who was curled up against the door, eyes closed and mouth open. "Did our silly sister wear you out?"

"*Nee*. She was fine."

After a few more miles passed, Graham pushed again. "Then, is it coming home that's got you out of sorts? Are you worried about seeing Gwen and Will again?"

The last thing he wanted to think about was either Gwen or Will. After everything that had happened on the train, and with Lucy, another couple's romance didn't seem that important to him.

But if he admitted that, he would sound even more despondent than he'd felt when he first left town. And that wasn't how he felt now. But he also wasn't eager to share his new feelings for Lucy. "I'm not worried about seeing either of them. How are they doing?"

Graham narrowed his eyes, as if he was trying to figure out if Calvin was being sarcastic or not. "I see that your time away did do you a world of good. Gwen and Will seem happy together, though Gwen did walk over and talk to Loyal and me the other day."

"About what?"

"You," Graham said flatly. "She was wondering how you were doing. I'm getting the sense that she doesn't care for feeling so guilty."

"I don't know what to say to that."

"You're a better man than I am, then. She seems like a terribly selfish girl, to be asking after you, after she near broke your heart."

"It wasn't that broken."

"You could have fooled me," Loyal said. "For weeks after Gwen wrote you that note, you moped around the farm like your world had ended."

He had moped. So much so, he was now embarrassed about his actions. "When I was out of town, I discovered my world didn't end after all," he joked.

Graham added, "For the record, I've never seen Will happier. He positively preens like a rooster whenever she is on his arm. Some people are saying a wedding will be happening between the two of them sooner than later."

"Gwen made no secret about wanting to marry—"

"*You*," Loyal interrupted harshly. "She had always said she wanted to marry you."

"Things—and people—change."

"At least she landed on her feet."

Calvin knew their words were not being fair to Gwen. Though he'd certainly been upset about her moving on so quickly to Will, now that he'd gained some perspective, Calvin couldn't say he'd been completely surprised. "I'm just fine, too, you know. You both can stop feeling sorry for me. And, I hope, we can drop this subject."

"Don't worry," Loyal said with a grin. "We're getting closer to home."

"Yep," Graham added. "Before you know it, we'll all be back at work in the fields, and your trip to Indianapolis will be a faded memory."

Calvin nodded, though he knew deep inside that he was not going to be able to forget everything.

Even if he wanted to, Calvin knew he would never forget the pretty blond woman with copper-colored eyes and a dimple in one cheek.

Who had enjoyed her day at the zoo with the kind of exuberance that rivaled Katie's. Who had gone without regular meals through power outages and foreign train stations with a calm acknowledgment.

And who had also known heartbreak, but she'd elected to help her cousin instead of dwell on the pain.

And who'd run out of his life over a misunderstanding about a horse.

Though he'd let her leave, he knew he was always going to remember her. No matter how hard he might try, he was never going to forget Lucy Troyer.

Then, like a bolt of lightning had just hit him, he re-membered once again . . . he still had her journal.

Chapter 12

"Lucy! You're here!" Mattie exclaimed, all smiles as her mother, Lucy's Aunt Jenna, led Lucy through the front door after a long embrace. "I can't believe you finally made it."

Lucy rushed to Mattie's side. As she did, she quickly took notice of her cousin's pale skin and the new lines around her eyes. The stress of the past month had already taken its toll on her body.

"*Finally* is right," she said with a smile before enveloping her cousin in a gentle hug. "For a while there, I wasn't sure if I was ever going to see your front door."

"I was thinking the same thing," Mattie replied. "Mamm and I must have looked at the clock a thousand times, wondering if you'd ever make it here."

"I've had a time of it. But it doesn't matter. I would have

gone through much worse in order to see you. Besides, you did the same for me, and more than once."

A new awareness entered Mattie's eyes as she looped her hand around Lucy's elbow. "Indeed, I did."

"I've never forgotten how much I appreciated you coming to see me after Paul died," Lucy said.

"Well, of course I would be there."

"I feel the same way now. It is a blessing to have the chance to help you."

A shadow entered Mattie's gaze. "I wish it wasn't for this reason."

"I know. But we'll get through it."

As Mattie led her into the front room, Lucy felt her cousin's eyes on her. She felt like she was getting inspected. "Well, how do I look?" she teased.

"Much better." Mattie tilted her head. "Especially given your trip here. I've been imagining the worst. It had to have been difficult, sitting by yourself for hours and hours on the train, and then later in the train terminal."

"It wasn't so bad."

"No?" She paused. "Hmm. Now that I think of it, whenever you left a message on the phone line you didn't sound too aggrieved."

"The train breaking down and the storms were scary, but the whole time wasn't a trial."

"I'm so glad."

Lucy was relieved Mattie didn't need to ask more questions, because she knew exactly why things hadn't been as bad as they could have been—because she'd been with Calvin Weaver.

As she thought of him and his sister, Lucy knew she would always be grateful for their companionship. For a few hours, she'd thought of herself as a woman again, not just the shell of one.

Actually, she had begun to think that the Lord had known exactly what He'd been doing when He had placed her in Calvin's company. He had encouraged her to have fun, and to think in the present.

Being with them had felt so freeing. For a brief time, no one was telling her what to do. Or asking about Paul.

No one was causing her to remember things she didn't want to. Or asking her to help mind her brothers and sisters. No work had begged for her attention. Instead, the journey's time had been all her own. A true gift.

Yes, her day with them had been wonderful . . . until she'd witnessed his temper.

"Well, you're here now, and that is all that matters," Aunt Jenna said as she bustled out of the kitchen, a dish towel in one hand, a mug of hot tea in the other. "Lucy, dear, it is time you did some relaxin' just like our Mattie here. Now, take a seat and sip some tea, why don't you?"

Lucy took the mug from her aunt and inhaled deeply. The spicy orange-cinnamon aroma smelled like heaven. But she still felt obligated to remind her that she hadn't come to Jacob's Crossing simply to relax. "I came to help, Aunt Jenna, not be waited on."

"Oh, don't you worry. I'll make sure you are put to work tomorrow," she said with a wink and a smile. "But you can't work and catch up with Mattie at the same time. Tonight will be a time to talk and enjoy each other's company, *jah*?"

"*Jah,*" Mattie said instantly. "I must admit that I'm terribly interested in all that you've been doing."

Before Lucy could utter a word, Aunt Jenna nodded her approval. "That's settled, then. While you two catch up, I'll bring you some snacks. Are you hungry, Lucy?"

"I am." Then, noticing her wrinkled dress with some dismay, she murmured, "But soon, I'm afraid, I'm going to need to take a hot shower and get to bed."

"We can offer you a bed and shower," Mattie replied with a smile, "but not yet. First, let's go to my sitting room and visit. I'm in no mood to let you out of my sight."

They walked through the entryway, past the quiet family room. After crossing another threshold, they entered a beautiful room, lit with two kerosene lamps. One whole side was composed of sparkling clean glass, while another had windows that were open. The warm spring breeze fluttered through the screens, filling the room with the blissful aroma of fresh flowers and cut grass.

Even after they took a seat, Mattie still held her arm. Lucy used the opportunity to take another look at her cousin.

Careful inspection revealed faint smudges under her eyes. She also seemed to hold herself stiffly, as if she was in pain. And underneath her cousin's bright smile and positive attitude lay something that Lucy could sense . . . a wealth of worries.

It was recognizable. Lucy herself had practiced that smile a lot during her marriage with Paul.

Mattie was not all right at all.

Moments later, Aunt Jenna carried in a finely crafted

wooden tray loaded with a bowl of berries and two plates of zucchini bread. "Here you two girls go," she said. "You enjoy, and relax. I'll go put your bag in your bedroom, Lucy."

Lucy stood. "Aunt Jenna, I'll do that."

"*Nee*. I will," she said airily as she left the room.

"Tell me about your trip," Mattie said when they were alone again. "What, exactly, caused your train to stop running?"

"I'm not precisely sure. It had an electrical problem or some such thing." Lucy paused to sip her delicious tea. "At first, I was scared. The rain was pouring, and thunder and lightning ran across the sky. The lights in our car kept going off."

"Lucy! And with you traveling alone, too!" Mattie set a thick slice of the moist bread on her plate and pushed it her way. "I bet you were terribly afraid."

After taking a bite, Lucy spoke. "I was, at first. But then I soon realized that the only thing to do was make the best of it. Panicking and fretting didn't solve any problems."

"So what did you do? Crochet?"

"*Nee!*" Lucy replied with a laugh. "At first it was too dark to do much, and then I started talking to an Amish man and his sister."

"Truly?" Her cousin mused. "I'm surprised about that, I must say. I didn't think you ever spoke to men, especially to strange ones."

"I usually don't, but he was friendly . . . and then it turned out that we had something in common."

"Oh?"

"He was from right here in Jacob's Crossing."

Mattie's look of surprise mirrored the feelings Lucy had fostered. "Who is it?"

"Calvin Weaver."

"Oh my word." Mattie leaned forward, her eyes bright. "Lucy, our families have lived next to each other for years."

"That's what he said. I still can't believe the coincidence."

Looking at Lucy closely, Mattie said, "So tell me. How did you two get along?"

"At first, things were a little uncomfortable. He's kind of a gregarious sort, and as you know, I am not."

"All the boys in his family are," Mattie said. "Though I would have to say that Calvin is the most outgoing. Loyal is slightly more serious; and Graham, well, Graham is a more introspective sort of person," she added with a secretive smile. Playfully, Mattie nudged her. "Well, don't be shy, now. What did you and Calvin talk about?"

"This and that."

"Such as . . ."

"We just talked, I guess. About our families some."

"Did you tell him about Paul?"

"Of course not. I didn't even tell him I had been married." Mattie raised her brows.

Lucy rushed to explain. "There was no need, you know. It's not like my past matters to him."

Over the rim of her mug, Mattie's eyes twinkled. "Perhaps you two will spend more time together here."

"I don't think so." Her feelings for Calvin were too confusing. The last thing she wanted was to see him again.

"We are neighbors. Of course your paths are bound to cross."

"He is not the reason I came to Ohio," she said firmly, gently wrapping an arm around her cousin's shoulders, enveloping her in a loose hug. "You are the person I want to spend time with."

"All right." Mattie clasped one of Lucy's hands.

Lucy wrapped her other palm around Mattie's, completely covering her hand. Oh, but Mattie felt so fragile and weak.

A lump formed in her throat. This girl was so different from the Mattie she'd known and loved every summer and Christmas when their families got together. That Mattie was boisterous and fun, almost a practical joker. Always the center of attention, whether she wanted to be or not.

This Mattie was quieter. Right then and there, Lucy made it her goal to help her cousin get back her old spark. "We are going to be busy, Mattie," she said gently. "In between your doctors' appointments and chemotherapy treatments, I'm going to make you laugh."

The muscles in her throat worked as Mattie obviously tried to keep her voice light. "You may regret your vow."

"Why is that?"

"I'm afraid I haven't been the easiest patient. I've been moody and sullen." With a thump, Mattie set her mug down. "At times, I fear my parents have not known what to do with me."

"If you were easy, you wouldn't be Mattie."

When her cousin's expression turned shocked, then offended, then very slowly turned to a spark of amusement, Lucy leaned back on the couch and grinned in relief.

Yes, getting Mattie through this difficult time was going to take all of her energy and a whole lot of prayer. But perhaps they would be successful.

It was just as well she wouldn't be seeing Calvin Weaver again. She had no time for him.

No time at all.

Chapter 13

John held out his hands to prevent the woman from knocking straight into him. "Hey," he said. "Look out, now."

His touch startled her. With a frown, she froze, and finally looked up from her cell phone.

And that's when he noticed her eyes were . . . violet? Who had violet eyes?

"Oh my gosh! Did I just walk right into you? I'm so sorry."

Her voice was musical. Slightly southern sounding. His mouth went dry. But because he was way too old for such nonsense, he dropped his hands and stepped a good three steps backward. "It's all right. I just didn't want you to get hurt." When she blinked at him and smiled slightly, he shook himself and tried to sound reasonable. Not smitten. "I mean, you probably shouldn't text and walk. At the same time. You're liable to run into someone."

Great, now he couldn't even form complete sentences.

Closing her phone, she shook her head in obvious frustration. With the motion, her short hair, as brown as a Hershey bar, shifted and flickered in the sunlight. Catching his attention. "This thing. My niece keeps trying to teach me how to use that predictive text. But no matter how hard I try, I can't do it right."

"It takes some practice."

Gazing at him with wide eyes, she asked, "Do you know how to do it?"

"Ah, not well enough to teach you."

"Oh. That's really too bad."

Yes. It *was* too bad. He was attracted to her and didn't have a single reason to keep the conversation going. But he could try. Holding out his hand, he introduced himself. "I'm John Weaver."

"Jayne Donovan." She smiled, revealing beautiful white teeth. The perfect match to her beautiful eyes. Her hand was slim and cool in his.

He stopped himself from rubbing his thumb over her smooth skin.

Oh, brother. John felt his cheeks heat. "I just moved here."

"Why?"

Who asked questions like that? "I once lived here. I decided to come back." Yep, that was definitely the short answer.

"Going home again, huh?"

"No. Well, maybe." How did he explain how it felt to be living in his childhood home? To be back in an Amish home . . . and though he loved his sister-in-law and her family dearly, he knew, without a doubt, that in time he would have to get out of there.

She smiled again. This time, he noticed lines around her eyes and mouth. She was older than he'd thought.

And then he caught himself again. "I should probably get going."

"All right." She bit her bottom lip. "And . . . John?"

"Yeah?"

"I'm sorry I almost ran into you. I should have been paying more attention."

"Hey, if you hadn't, we wouldn't have met." Mentally, he rolled his eyes. Could he sound any cheesier if he tried?

"I work at the library, if you ever need a book."

She turned and walked away before he could process that. No, Jayne Donovan walked away before *he* could think of anything else to say.

And he couldn't help standing there for a moment and watching her walk.

"Move along now, son," a man said, passing him. "You're making a spectacle of yourself, standing and gawking like you are."

Embarrassed, John darted into the first place of business he could find—a somewhat down-on-its-luck donut shop.

A man who looked to be seventy years old stood behind the counter, eyeing him with interest as he approached. "Can I help you?"

John didn't really want anything, but he was obligated to get something. "How fresh is your coffee?"

"Fresh." The man glared at him—almost looking like he'd love for John to pick a fight.

"I'll have a cup of coffee and one of those glazed donuts."

"Three dollars."

As John pulled out three singles, he looked the old guy over. The man was only a few inches over five feet. He had a stooped posture and dark eyes and was almost bald. "Thanks," he said when the man handed him a cardboard cup and donut in a white sack.

"You new here in town?"

"I am, more or less. I'm moving back."

"You look just like Jacob Weaver."

"That's because I'm his brother."

Something flickered in the old guy's eyes. After a moment's hesitation, he walked around the bakery case and gestured to a table. "Have a seat."

The man looked a little too intent. "Thanks, but I've got to get going . . ."

"Where?" Before John could make up something, the man pointed one bony finger at the table again. "Have a seat. We'll catch up."

This time John sat. "Do I know you?"

"I don't know. But I sure knew your father." After a pause, he held out a hand. "Name's Amos House."

"House?"

Amos winked as he sat. "Yep, just like a home, but not. Now, tell me what you've been doing for so long."

Fingers curved around the cup of coffee, John started

talking. And before he knew it, he felt completely at ease for pretty much the first time since he'd returned to Jacob's Crossing.

Once every few weeks, Calvin or one of his brothers took their mother to the Wal-Mart in Middlefield. No matter whose turn it was, the chore was always looked upon as a labor of love.

Their mother loved Wal-Mart. Her eyes positively lit up at the sight of the giant store.

Because of that—and because she'd always been so eager to make her children happy—they made sure one of them was always available to take her there.

Calvin jingled Beauty's reins as their sturdy horse plodded along the back roads to the supercenter. Beside him, his mother was continuing her efforts to fill him in on everything he'd missed while he was in Indiana.

"So, on Sunday, we had church at the Yoders', and it was a *verra* fine service," his mother said. "And you should see their new barn! It is a fair sight to see."

"It's made of metal, ain't so?"

"It is, indeed. And so very sparkling and new. They put windows high in the ceiling, too. As we prayed, it felt as if rays of sunlight beamed right down on us, lighting our way. Oh, Calvin. I wish you could have been there."

"I'll be there next time they host."

"I hope so." She worried her bottom lip. "Or maybe you should take a look at it sooner than later. That barn was really pretty, Calvin. I was most impressed with it, actually. If we had the need for a new barn, I would tell you boys to build it like the Yoders'."

"We don't have that need," he said quickly before she could warm up to the subject. Their mother loved new things, new gadgets, new anything.

"Oh, I know. I'm just saying . . . if we did need a new barn—"

"Which we do not—"

"I would want one just like the Yoders'."

Calvin looked at his mother fondly. Of his two parents, she'd always been the more adventurous one. Unlike his father, who had enjoyed a peaceful and steady way of life, his mother yearned for all things new. She found excitement in almost everything. Even now he was amazed at how well she did as a widow. Though she missed his father terribly, he never witnessed her looking at the world through a disappointed haze. Instead, she seemed determined to make each day count.

As he should, too, he realized with some dismay. For the weeks before his trip, he'd hardly been aware of anything besides his own heartbreak.

But the trip home had changed his perspective. "I'll go to the Yoders' soon and give it a look."

"I hope you will. They will be happy to see you, I am sure. Why, Corrine and Thomas both asked about you during lunch."

"That was kind of them."

"Oh, they were just worried, on account of your moping. Thomas, especially, was worried you were taking Gwen's rejection of you awfully hard."

Leave it to his mother to put things as plainly as possible. "I'm thankful for their concern."

As they approached a traffic light, Calvin reined in Beauty and watched for oncoming traffic. When the light turned green, he pulled out and turned left. Just a few hundred yards up ahead, the bright blue-and-white sign for the Wal-Mart loomed. "We're almost at the store," he murmured. "Here's the Arby's and the KFC."

"One day we should try out those places." Craning forward, she pointed to the area off to the left of the store, where all the buggies were hitched, some in the tan enclosure built specifically for the horses and buggies. "Look, Calvin. There's a fair amount of folks already here."

"It will be a crowded shopping day, to be sure."

"Oh, *jah*! It will be a mighty good time to visit with friends."

Calvin grinned. Yet again, his mother had taken his comment and turned it upside down. "Do you have a list today, or are you just going to explore?" he teased. It had become something of a family joke to tease their mother about her behavior when the store had held the opening celebration.

While their father had wanted nothing to do with the opening of the gargantuan place, their mother had counted the days. Calvin and Graham had ended up taking her to the store on Grand Opening Day. They'd dealt with the crowds and the noise for more than two hours while their mother carefully inspected every aisle . . . and tried all the free food samples.

Time and again, they'd lost sight of her as she'd darted off to inspect new gadgets and cleaning products, and smiled at the blocks of ice in the freezer section—all while pushing her metal cart up and down the aisles with the resolve of an explorer of old.

Now, though quite some time had passed, she still blushed. "Oh, Calvin. Will you ever let me forget that day?"

"I'm sure I will . . . one day." After they shared a smile, he asked, "Do you have a lot to shop for?"

"I do have a list," she said primly. "But . . . I will probably look around for a little while, too."

Calvin wisely said nothing about that. After guiding Beauty to one of the many hitching posts, he set the brake and helped his mother hop down. Then, after a few minutes of taking care of the horse, they walked toward one of the main entrances.

"I'll meet you here in a bit," his mother said as she selected a grocery cart, her eyes already jumping from one brightly organized display to the next.

"Take your time, Mamm," he murmured as he tried to get acclimated to the fresh burst of air-conditioning, the bright lights, and the amazing amount of colors and noises surrounding them.

Over to the side, near the fabric section, Calvin recognized some of his mother's dear friends. One of them was waving her over, and she was scurrying toward them like it had been weeks since they'd seen each other instead of just days.

Calvin hid a smile as one of them held up a flyer advertising all the store's specials.

Yes, today was going to be another lengthy trip.

He waved to her friends, then darted off in the opposite

direction, on the off chance that they would try to circle him in. The last thing he wanted was to hear the latest gossip about Gwen and Will. After he passed two aisles of sporting goods, he spied a display of fishing lures. Looking at them was as good an activity as any to pass the time.

And then he spied her. On the other side of a paper towel display. In the pet-food aisle.

Calvin dropped the box of fishing lures he was holding and craned his neck, squinting a bit, just to make sure his eyes weren't deceiving him.

But as her head lifted and he caught the angle of her fine jaw, Calvin knew there was no mistake at all.

Right there, standing a mere ten feet away, in the middle of the biggest Wal-Mart Supercenter in the region . . . was Lucy Troyer. His heart thumped as he recalled their argument. And the cool way she'd treated him after.

But overriding all of that was the guilt he felt—he'd never given her back her diary. He definitely should have done that.

Of course, he should have never opened it. Or read portions of what was inside. Or stewed on it.

Or even—perhaps just a little—judged her for what she wrote.

Yes, he had already done much to feel guilty about. Until he got his feelings and emotions under control, Calvin knew the right thing to do would be to walk away from her. Pretend their paths hadn't crossed.

Pretend he'd never seen her.

But the pull he felt toward her prevented all of that. No, he could no more ignore her than he could walk away from the store without his mother. It wasn't who he was. With that in mind, he called out to her and hoped for the best.

"Lucy!"

Lucy abruptly turned to whoever was calling her name. "Calvin? My goodness. I'm shocked to see you! Whatever are you doing here?"

"I was going to ask you that same thing," he said, sauntering over.

Warring emotions flowed through her as he approached. She was so glad to see Calvin—but afraid to talk with him. She recalled his temper. And her lack of willingness to listen to his apology.

She remembered the way he'd looked after her in the train station in Toledo. And the patience he'd had for little Katie.

And the warmth she'd felt when she'd spied his regard for her.

And the chill she'd felt when she'd seen his scorn.

While those mixed emotions spun in her mind, Lucy couldn't help but stare at him. Reacquainting herself with him, her eyes leapt from one part of his body to the next, automatically taking stock.

He was as handsome as ever. His blue eyes clear and merry. His light blond hair was as thick and straight as she remembered. And just as in need of fingertips to smooth it out. And that slight bump in the line of his nose reminded her that he still wasn't perfect.

Yes, Calvin looked much the same, only better. He wore a fresh white shirt and black suspenders. Black pants and boots. His hat was straw.

He looked much like every other Amish man, but to her, so much more. There was a sparkle in his eyes that she had once found comfort in. His smile was just as wide, his teeth just as white. But it was his natural exuberance that drew her to him like little else ever had.

He stopped a few feet away from her, as if he feared getting too close. "Are you here on your own?"

"No, I'm with my Aunt Jenna. My uncle is with Mattie. She had to see the *doktah*. We're getting a few things done until it is time to pick them up. What about you?"

"My mother wanted to pick up some bulk foods, but she got sidetracked by her friends. So now I'm wandering around." Now that he was standing next to her, he leaned a little closer, closing the space between them.

Now she smelled the lingering scent of soap on his skin, and a faint aroma of leather and horse. Her mouth went dry.

If Calvin noticed the way she was affected by him, he gave no sign. Just like they saw each other all the time, he asked, "Care to wander around a bit with me?"

With effort, she made herself remember his scowl. Made herself remember his clenched fists. Though it was almost painful to do so, she retreated. "I had better not."

"Please? I promise, I just want to visit with you for a bit." His voice was gentle, patient. Like he had all the time in the day for her. When she raised her eyes to his, the faint laugh lines around his eyes deepened. "I promise— that's all," he murmured.

Say no, she cautioned herself. *Say no and be safe.* But her tongue—the traitor that it was—answered before she could follow her own advice. "Well, then . . . all right."

Calvin's eyes lit up. Then, by mutual consent, they started walking. They walked past the pet-food aisle, into the lawn-and-garden area. Usually, Lucy knew she would have been interested in the multitude of gardening products and trays of fresh flowers. But not now. Now she neither smelled the scents of the many roses nor noticed the blue begonias.

No, she noticed only his square jaw and the blue of his eyes.

When he noticed her inspecting him, he smiled. "So, how is your cousin? I haven't heard much from Graham."

"Mattie is having a time of it, I'm afraid. She's scared but doesn't want to burden anyone. Because of that, sometimes I think she's in more pain than she needs to be, simply because she doesn't want to ask either her parents or me for more medicine or help."

"Perhaps you will learn to predict her needs. Or she will learn to accept your help."

"I hope so. Uncle Ben and Aunt Jenna have been beside themselves with worry. They fret, then ask Mattie things she can't answer. Next thing you know, she begins to get stressed and my aunt and uncle get perturbed. It's an uneasy situation."

"I imagine so."

"What of you? How is Katie? And your brothers?"

"Katie is fine. As bossy and chatty as ever. And my brothers are well enough. The same." Calvin paused, his attention momentarily diverted by the array of televisions in front of them. Each showed the same picture, of a man on a golf course. When the player in the bright orange shirt hit the ball and the crowd surrounding him clapped, Calvin whistled low. "I'm sorry. I've always fancied golf. I can't seem to help myself."

"Have you played?"

"Once or twice with John." His eyes darted to the television screens again. His voice grew softer. "There's something about simply being outside in nature, walking along in the silence, only thinking about trying to hit a tiny white ball, that I enjoy. You should play one day. You'd like it, I feel sure."

He felt sure? Until this very moment, she'd never imagined playing golf. Actually, she'd never even thought about golf or golf courses at all. But now, seeing the wonder in Calvin's eyes, she began to imagine that she, too, could try something new. "Perhaps one day I'll get the opportunity."

"I hope you shall. But for now, we had best walk on. Now, tell me . . . have you thought of our trip to the zoo much?"

"I have." *Only all the time.* "You?"

"I have." His expression turning solemn, he added, "And I've thought much about what happened afterward. You know I was only worried about the horse, don't you?" Before she could answer, he added quickly, "Lucy, I promise, it's not in my nature to be an angry or violent man."

Lucy looked at his face, thought about his behavior the whole time they had been together on the train. Recalled how patient he'd been with his sister. And with her. And slowly let herself believe that maybe—just maybe—his temper had been a one-time thing. "Calvin. You were so very angry."

"I know. And I'm sorry I frightened you," he added quickly as his eyes turned pleading. "But, Lucy, he was slowly killing his horse. And that poor mare had no escape. Someone had to stand up for it. Even if it did no good, someone had to care enough to at least try."

A lump formed in her throat as she processed his words. And then finally it clicked. Calvin had been trying to prevent abuse—not perpetrate it.

How different her life might have been if someone had come to her aid.

"Perhaps . . . perhaps, I overreacted. If I did, I'm sorry," she murmured as they headed back toward the front of the store.

Pure relief entered his eyes. "So, we're better? You understand?"

Her emotions were so high, she could only nod.

"Ah, Lucy! I found you!" Aunt Jenna called out from a bevy of ladies. "And you found Calvin. How nice." Jenna beckoned them toward her. "Calvin, how are you?"

"I am well, thank you."

More ladies approached them. With her hand resting on Lucy's shoulder, Aunt Jenna said proudly, "Everyone, this is my niece Lucy. She's come to help with Mattie's treatments for a month."

"I'm pleased to meet all of you."

Next to her, Calvin said, "Lucy, this is my *mamm*, Mary Weaver."

"It is nice to meet you, too."

"I heard about your train ride," Mrs. Weaver said. "I'm glad you and Calvin had each other for company."

"And John. And Katie." Lucy looked at Calvin and couldn't help but smile. "I was thankful for them all."

Mrs. Weaver chuckled. "That's terribly kind of you. You must be a mighty nice woman, Lucy. Our Katie can try the patience of us all sometimes."

Darting a look Calvin's way, Lucy said, "I can see how that would be true."

More ladies approached, teasing Jenna and Mary, and began chatting with Calvin. Lucy scanned the area, wondering just how many Amish ladies could be in one Wal-Mart.

And then she noticed a girl about her age, standing off to the side. Watching them.

She looked away, trying to focus on the conversation. But then she glanced the girl's way again. No, she hadn't been mistaken. The girl was definitely staring, and her expression was thunderous. Lucy raised her chin and looked straight back.

Calvin looked at her curiously. "Lucy? What is it?"

"I'm not sure. That girl seems to be staring at us. "

He shrugged. "The English do like to stare."

"No, it's more than that."

Still not taking his eyes from her, he said, "Well, you are very pretty. Perhaps that's why she's looking."

Their eyes met. Her stomach did a little flip. Once again, she felt the same pull toward him that she had at the zoo.

Until his mother lifted her head and stiffened as well. "Oh, dear," she said.

Calvin finally looked. Then sighed. "That girl is Gwen

Kent," he said after a moment. "She and I . . . we were sweethearts. Once."

Unable to stop herself, Lucy said curiously, "Is she mad at you?"

"Oh, I wouldn't say that."

"Nothing's wrong with Calvin," his mother said. "But that Gwen, well . . . she near broke his heart."

"Mamm," he warned.

"It's true," another lady murmured. "Everyone, including Calvin here, thought they would be planning a wedding soon. But instead, Gwen's eye strayed. Next thing we all knew, she was keeping company with Will."

"It wasn't quite like that," Calvin said, looking like he wished he were anywhere but where he was. "Gwen and Will, um, fell in love in spite of themselves."

"Hmmph," his mother said.

Lucy felt a chill to her bones. It seemed she hadn't been the only person to be taken in by false promises before. "I'm terribly sorry."

Calvin shrugged and turned away. "Oh, it's not such a big thing now."

Lucy said nothing, but couldn't forget the look in his eyes when he'd revealed that Gwen had once been his girl.

Oh, but the Lord had a sense of humor. Not only was He putting Calvin in her life again, but He was placing his sweetheart there as well, just to remind Lucy not to trust herself.

Or men.

Not even Calvin Weaver.

Chapter 14

From the moment he'd met Amos, John knew he'd made a friend. A very good friend.

The second time they'd talked, when he'd confided to the old guy that he was uncomfortable living on the farm, Amos offered a solution. Amos wanted a partner. Actually, he wanted someone to take over his business.

"All I want to do is make donuts, John," he'd groused. "I'm gonna go nuts if I have to sit back behind that forsaken counter for one more day."

"I can sit there all day. I make a decent cup of coffee, too," he'd said.

After a brief conversation about money, the deal was done.

The offer of becoming partners in the donut shop

should have taken a lot of thought and consideration. But John knew it felt right.

So he'd accepted Amos's offer to live above the donut shop, and now worked side by side with the elderly man, learning the business, and enjoying his company.

Things with his brother's family were going well, too. Little by little, their conversations were less stilted. Mary now invited him over for dinner on Fridays. Calvin, Loyal, and Graham seemed to accept him in their lives . . . even if he wasn't Amish. Katie, of course, had made his life wonderful. Every time they saw each other, she greeted him with hugs and kisses, and big happy smiles.

In town, he was also becoming more comfortable. He was making a few friends.

And then there was Jayne Donovan. Since their run-in, he'd seen her one other time. And though they didn't have a date or anything planned, he knew there was an attraction between them that couldn't be denied. Every time he was near her, he couldn't help but stare at those unusual eyes of hers.

Taking out a fresh towel, he started wiping down one of the empty bakery cases.

And then thought about Jayne some more. Yep. One of these days, he was going to have to ask her out. Maybe he'd take her into Chagrin Falls—it was only a thirty-minute drive. He could take her out to dinner . . . they could walk around the square, look at the falls.

She could smile at him . . . and he could think about kissing her good night—

"Excuse me? Are you working?"

Slowly, he got to his feet from where he knelt. "Obviously," he replied, smiling to take the sting out of his remark. He'd always had the tendency to be too cheeky.

The Amish woman's eyes widened as he stood up, then she carefully stepped a little closer to her son standing next to her. He was a handsome boy, on the verge of manhood. Probably twelve, or thereabouts.

"May I help you?" he asked.

"You may," she said primly. "We need a dozen donuts, please."

He washed his hands quickly, then grabbed a box. "Any special kind?"

She bit her lip, just as if she was making the biggest decision of the day. Finally she looked at him. "All glazed, please."

Her eyes were a pale green, the exact same color as the boy's. Leaning his elbows on the counter, he smiled at the boy. "Are you sure? We have lots of other kinds. Lemon filled, cream cakes . . ."

Her eyes widened, then she shook her head. "No, glazed will do fine."

Agreeably, he arranged the twelve donuts in a box, then smiled at the boy. "When you order twelve you get a baker's dozen. Do you want your thirteenth now?"

His eyes lit up. "Can I, Mamm?"

Again, John watched her make the stupendous decision. But instead of feeling irritated, he became amused. She really was a cute thing. "All right," she finally said. "You worked hard at the store today."

"What kind do you want?" John asked.

"Chocolate," the boy said.

After John gave him it, the boy whispered and pointed to the window.

The lady nodded and watched him leave before turning to John. "How much?"

"Six-fifty." While he waited for her to get out her wallet, John said, "Good-looking boy you have."

She handed him a five. "*Danke.* I mean, thank you."

"I know *Danke.* I grew up Amish," he said, surprising himself. He couldn't remember the last person he'd told out of the blue like that. "I see he has your eyes. Is he your only one?"

"Yes." She smiled. "My Abel is a wonderful-*gut* son. He's been a great help to me ever since my husband passed on to heaven."

"I'm sorry for your loss."

"I am, too." She shrugged. "But unfortunately, I lost my husband almost eight years ago. It's been some time."

"And you haven't remarried?"

She shook her head, then stilled. Perhaps noticing, as John was, that the conversation was bordering on awkward.

He handed her the box, neatly taped up. "Here you go. I hope you'll come back."

"Are you new here?"

"In a way. I'm John Weaver, Jacob Weaver's younger brother, if you know his family. I moved away twenty years ago, but I'm back."

"To stay?"

"Yes."

She looked at him again, then finally smiled. "Then perhaps I will see you again. Abel and I enjoy these donuts."

"Especially the glazed?"

Her cheeks pinkened just like a girl's. "Yes," she murmured before turning away.

John watched her walk over to where her son was chatting with two other boys. She smiled. And then, to his amusement, she opened the box and offered the boys donuts, too.

John was . . . charmed.

She was fresh and sweet and had the prettiest eyes he'd ever seen. And though she knew his name, and he knew Abel's, John realized he didn't know her name. He really should have asked.

"Mattie? Mattie, can you hear me? It's time to wake up for a bit."

Mattie opened her eyes, looked at Lucy, and groaned. "How can this medicine be making me better? This morning, I feel ten times worse than I did at the medical center."

"The nurses warned that might be the case," Lucy said as she perched on the side of the bed. She held up a cup of ice water. "Do you want a sip?"

Mattie didn't want a thing. She wanted to curl up in a ball and wish her troubles away. Have a good cry. But even in the weak condition she was in, she knew that wouldn't help. Nothing good ever came from hiding and pretending nothing was wrong. She'd discovered that when she'd felt a lump under her arm and had ignored it.

Gingerly, she sat up and tried to smile. Though it embarrassed her, she let Lucy hold her cup for her as she sipped once, then swallowed again. The icy water did taste wonderful on her parched tongue. She swallowed again, but too fast and choked.

"Easy now," Lucy murmured. "Take small sips."

Mattie did as she bid. When the cup was half empty, she looked at Lucy and smiled.

Lucy returned her weak smile tenfold. "See, Mattie, things are going to be all right. Slowly but surely, we're going to get through this. I'm sure of it."

"*Slowly* is right," she mumbled.

Doubt clouded Lucy's caramel eyes for a moment before she beamed again. "Come now. We must look on the bright side, *jah*? You got through your first treatment!" Hardly skipping a beat, Lucy started smoothing Mattie's fluffed pillows and yellow basket–patterned quilt. "That cancer isn't going to have a chance."

"I hope so," she replied, though mentally she rolled her eyes. Yesterday, when they'd first put the medicine in her IV tube, she'd been scared to death. When she'd felt the cold liquid pour into her veins, she'd braced herself for pain. But none came, perhaps because of the many pills she was taking now to fight off everything from pain to nausea to sleeplessness.

However, today nothing seemed right. She felt achy and worn-out. So, so tired.

Leaning closer, Lucy carefully wrapped her hands around Mattie's. Warming them. "Please stay positive, Mattie. You're a fighter, and you're going to win this battle, I just know it."

"A fighter, hmm?" Mattie mused. "I never thought of myself in that way."

"It's about time you did. Now, are you ready to walk down the hall and use the restroom?"

"I suppose."

Over the next hour, Lucy held her cousin steady as she walked down the hall, took care of her needs, and brushed her hair.

When Lucy offered to bring her some toast in bed, Mattie shook her head. "I can sit in the family room, at least. Just help me get on a robe."

Finally, while sitting on the couch, armed with hot herbal tea and some dry toast, Mattie was just feeling almost like herself when the kitchen door opened. "Hello?" a male voice called out. "May I come in?"

With a glare, Lucy jumped to her feet.

Mattie laughed. Lucy looked so like an avenging angel. "It's just Graham, Lucy. Not a stranger."

"Graham?"

"Graham Weaver," Mattie explained. "You know. Calvin's younger brother."

He poked his head in. "May I come in?"

Lucy started toward the kitchen. "What do you want to do?" she whispered. "Do you want me to make him leave?"

"No." What her cousin didn't understand was that she and Graham had been friends for pretty much all their lives. "If he came to visit, I'd like to see him for a bit."

Before Lucy could say another word, Graham bounded forward. "Hello, Lucy," he said politely, then crossed the room to Mattie, a bouquet of tulips in his hand. "I brought you some flowers."

"So I see."

Looking pleased with himself, he said, "I thought you might want to see some spring flowers when you wake up in the mornings."

They were lovely. The eight blooms were a mixture of rose and violet and yellow, each one prettier than the last. "Nothing could brighten my day more," she said honestly.

Still hovering, Lucy stepped forward. "I'll put the tulips in water," Lucy offered.

"*Danke,*" Mattie said.

When they were alone, Graham pulled up a chair and sat next to her. Oh, but he looked so dear. And so ill at ease.

Turning serious, he said, "How are you doing?"

"Well enough, I suppose."

He shook his head. "Really?"

"Ah, we're telling the truth now, are we?" She shrugged. "I've been better."

"Mattie, are you in pain?"

"A little, but I don't need anything," she added when he looked like he was about to jump to his feet to get her help. "I mean beyond the flowers."

"I'll bring them to you all the time, then." His teasing smile let her know that she didn't need to take him seriously.

"There's no need for that. Just bring yourself. You know I value your friendship the most."

"You always have that," he said quietly as he reached out and took her hand. Like she was made of glass, he ran one finger along the black-and-blue marks. "Ah, Mattie. Look at that. You've got a good-sized bruise on your hand."

She pushed up her sleeve to show him another quarter-sized mark on the inside of her elbow, where they took so many blood samples. "I'm a regular pincushion these days, I'm afraid. I look ugly."

"Never that."

Graham's words were softly said, but there seemed to be a hint of something new, too. A deeper emotion, right under the surface.

As she sat by his side, sensing his warmth, that old, familiar feeling of fascination for Graham came rolling back. Years ago, back when they were barely thirteen or fourteen, she'd had a terrible crush on him. He'd been so cute, and a favorite with all the girls.

She, on the other hand, had been going through an awkward stage, all arms and legs. That, combined with her moony gaze, had worked against any hope of the two of them being together.

In what had felt like no time at all, Graham had looked beyond his gangly next-door neighbor. Instead, he'd spent all his energy flirting with just about every other girl in their circle of friends.

After a time, she'd shaken off her infatuation and had moved on. Content to only be friends, thankful to have a good friend in him.

But now, as he stared at her, she wondered what would happen if things changed between them. Would their relationship turn awkward? Hesitant? Or would it finally feel right . . . the way it was supposed to?

Graham blinked, then smoothed a wrinkle on his shirt. "What, Mattie? Do I have a spider on me or somethin'?"

"Definitely not! You know if you had a spider on you, I'd be squealing."

He laughed. "That's true. I've never met a woman so afraid of bugs. So . . . you okay?"

"*Jah*. My mind just drifted, I suppose. Thank you again for the flowers."

"Anytime." But there was still a new wariness about him.

"Tell me about your brothers," she murmured. "What's new with them?"

Relaxing against the cushion of the couch, Graham propped one foot over his opposite knee. "Quite a bit, actually. As you know, Calvin and Katie had a *gut* time on his trip to Indianapolis."

"I did hear that. And they brought home your uncle?"

"They did, indeed. John stayed with us for a bit, and now is living in town." He winked at Lucy, who was back at her post by the door. "Every day we hear new stories about that train ride." Her cousin squirmed.

"It was definitely an unusual day," she mumbled.

That surprised a chuckle from Mattie. "I can't believe you and Calvin were on the same train."

"It was certainly a twist of fate," Lucy agreed. "And, of course, Katie was with us."

Graham smiled at that. "Katie has a way of getting into the middle of every major event."

"She is a busy girl, that is for sure," Mattie mused. Darting another quick glance Lucy's way, she said, "I do hope Calvin will come over soon."

Sure enough, at the mention of Calvin's name, Lucy's cheeks pinkened.

Leaning forward, Graham reached for Mattie's hand and tucked it between his own work-roughened palms. "Calvin will stop by soon," he promised. "He's just been giving you some space."

"I've had plenty of that."

"Then I'll tell him it is all right to stop by. I know he wants to see you, Mattie. Every time I come home after seeing you, he asks how you are doing." Encompassing Lucy into his gaze, he added, "As a matter of fact, he asks how both of you are."

"Now, isn't that kind of him?" Mattie glanced Lucy's way again. Although her cousin looked to be studiously examining a cut on her finger, Mattie knew she was hanging on every word about Calvin. Looking back at Graham, she said, "I know Calvin and I are *gut* friends . . . but perhaps he wants to see someone else, too?"

His eyes lighting up, Graham nodded. "I would wager he does."

Lucy bit her lip. "I don't know about that. We didn't part on the best of terms."

"That's easy enough to fix, don'tcha think?" Mattie asked. Thinking of her cancer, and of the way it had snuck up on her and then taken over her life, she said, "I'm coming to learn that there's some things that are out of our hands. And some things that aren't too difficult to take charge of."

"And you think this is one of those things?" Lucy asked, her tone tinged with sarcasm.

"Absolutely," Mattie said.

Actually, she knew for a fact that patching things up with Calvin wouldn't be too difficult at all. Only things involved there were words. Not needles or operations.

Or fear.

As if sensing an internal distress, Graham clasped her hand again and squeezed it gently. Grateful for his touch, Mattie smiled his way. Thank goodness for Graham. Thank goodness for good friends.

Chapter 15

John Weaver knew he was too old to be doing what he was doing—mooning about two women.

"John?" Amos called out, his voice as sharp and biting as a tack. "Are you ever going to help carry the trays inside, or do I need to get someone younger to help?"

Just to give the old guy grief, John said, "Definitely someone younger. Got anyone else in mind?"

"Unfortunately, no," he answered as John met him in the large kitchen at the back of the building.

"Guess I'll have to help you out, then . . ."

"Guess so. Pick up the tray and be smart about it."

Hiding a smile, John picked up the tray loaded with three dozen donuts and followed Amos into the front of the store, where the bakery cases were. Just as he prepared to slide the tray into the glass case, he noticed a pair of customers waiting by the front door. "We've got customers already."

Amos grunted. "No, *you* have customers. My day is almost done."

And with that, he disappeared back into the kitchen, leaving John to stride to the front and unlock the door. "Good morning, ladies," he said.

"Good morning. You kept us waiting long enough," the elder woman said.

As John turned away and walked back to the counter, he mentally rolled his eyes. Obviously, he was destined to be surrounded by grumpy old folks today! "What may I get you?" he asked as the door chimed, announcing the arrival of two more customers. Thank goodness he'd already brewed two pots of coffee; they were going to need it today.

The elderly lady gazed at the tray that John had just brought in. "This is it? All you have right now are glazed and chocolate-covered?"

"Cinnamon rolls are coming." That was, if Amos decided to bring them forward.

"I'll have two chocolate for now. And a cup of coffee."

As he rung the first pair up, he glanced at the new arrivals, and felt his heart jump. Jayne Donovan was standing there. Smiling at him.

He smiled right back.

"Stop standing around and smiling at women, John," Amos griped as he carried in a plate of ten cinnamon rolls. "You've got customers to attend to."

John ignored the old guy and smiled at Jayne. "Good morning."

"Hi, John," she said, her eyes sparkling. "I see you're pretty busy today."

"Well, I'm busy getting yelled at."

To his pleasure, she laughed. "I have to go right to work, so can I have one of those rolls to go?"

"Sure."

"I'll get it," Amos interjected. "You help the next folks."

With some surprise, John realized that while he'd been smiling at Jayne like a lovesick pup, even more people had come through the door. Including that woman. The Amish woman.

Unbidden, his mouth went dry. "*Gut matin,*" he murmured.

Her eyes widened and a beautiful sheen of roses lit her cheeks. "And *gut matin* to you, John. May I have a glazed donut?"

"Of course." As he handed her one, he looked behind her. "Your son isn't with you today?"

"*Nee.* He's at school." She paused, then handed him a dollar.

Their fingers touched as the money was exchanged. John was sure he was imagining things, but he could have sworn he felt a little spark between them.

Just as he was thinking about that, Jayne stepped into his line of vision. "John, I hope you have a good day. Bye!"

He lifted his hand and waved her off. "Come back soon," he said.

Behind him, Amos grunted. "Oh, brother."

John felt his cheeks heat. He didn't blame the old guy one bit. "Sorry."

"It's all right," Amos said, his eyes merry. "But there are still customers in line, Romeo."

John scowled, and would have said something, but just then he noticed the Amish woman was walking away. And he still didn't know her name!

Stepping out from around the counter, he walked quickly toward her. "Excuse me. Miss?"

She turned. "Yes?"

"What's your name?"

Behind him, Amos coughed.

"Mary," she murmured with a smile, before walking out the door.

Mary. Well, now. That suited her, he thought as he walked back to the counter. She really was lovely, and so peaceful looking.

Amos harrumphed. "John? You working?"

"Settle down," John snapped, then turned to the next customer. "May I help you?"

And so it continued, while in the back of his mind he wondered what the good Lord was up to. For twenty years, he'd had little to no interest in any woman. Now, all the sudden, he seemed to be attracted to two. One English, one Amish.

It seemed the Lord definitely had a sense of humor.

Another week had passed—and with it, another chemotherapy treatment. In between had been a blur of doctors' visits, blood tests, and nausea.

And, for Lucy, worry. She'd so wanted to help Mattie feel better, to help keep her spirits strong. But no matter what she did, her efforts paled in comparison to the sickness that had taken hold of her cousin's body. Mattie's skin was pallid and there were dark circles under her eyes.

But still she tried her best. "Things will get better, Mattie. I promise, they will."

"I doubt it."

"We can't give up hope, dear. Come, let's pray."

"Not now," she mumbled, just as her body was racked by fierce tremors. "Lucy, I don't know if I can do this anymore."

Lucy bit her bottom lip to keep her voice smooth and strong. And to hide her worry and anxiety. "You must."

"But the doctor didn't say it would be this bad."

"Ach. We both know it isn't the doctor who knows everything. It is the nurses, *jah*?"

Mattie shivered again. "What did the nurses say, then? I don't remember."

"They said this time the chemo might make you sick. They said, for a lot of patients, the second treatment is worse than the first."

"Then they were right about that."

Mattie wrapped her arms around herself as she curled up on the couch. "Lucy, I am sorry. I thought I would be a better patient for you."

"That is not why I came here, and you know it. I came to tend to you, not to sit and twiddle my thumbs."

A lone tear slipped down her sweet cousin's cheek as she looked her way. "I know you don't mind, but I hate the idea of you seeing me like this. All I seem to be able to do is shake and throw up. It's all awful."

It was awful, but not in the way Mattie thought. It was awful to see her dear cousin suffer so. "It's no worse than what you've done for me," she said quietly. "Remember when you came to help me cook?"

"Because your arm was in a cast?" Mattie nodded. "Of course."

"During that visit, you helped me more than I can say."

Mattie turned her way. "Ah, now I know you are feelin' flustered. Otherwise you wouldn't have spoken of that time."

Mattie was right. Rarely did Lucy ever choose to speak of her married life. And especially not the days when she'd been at her lowest. When Paul had made her life so miserable she'd wondered what had ever made her hope for a life next to Paul's side. "Though I may not talk of it, I haven't forgotten how good you were to me."

"How good was I?" Mattie mused weakly. "I never said a word to the rest of the family about just how bad he hurt you." After a moment, she added, "If I had, maybe he would've stopped."

Lucy knew full and well that Paul never would have stopped. "You didn't tell anyone because I asked you not to. Besides, what could you have done?" There had been no hope for any way out of her rocky marriage.

"My *daed* would've tried to help . . ."

Her uncle would have been no match for Paul's will—or for her marriage vows. Besides, no lecture from her relatives would've stopped what happened when she and Paul were alone. "Shhh, Mattie. Do not speak of it."

"But—"

"*Nee*. It's all over now. There's no need to worry yourself." She didn't want to talk about the past. Didn't want to have to say that she had been very aware that most people in their family and her friends had had an extremely good idea of what went on in her marriage.

After all, while Paul had done his worst in private, he'd been open about his lack of respect for her. It didn't matter who was around to witness his jabs—it was a rare day when she had ever been good enough for him.

Beside her Mattie shifted again. "I feel like my body's on fire."

"What can I do? Do you want some ice? Some cold compresses?"

"*Nee*. I'm sick and tired of ice."

"Water? Juice?" She thought hard. "I brought some sodas home from the store. Do you remember how last time the soda helped your stomach?"

"I don't want anything to drink."

"Okay, then."

Minutes passed. Almost a half hour.

Then, just when Lucy wondered if Mattie had finally begun to sleep, Mattie spoke. "Lucy, would you mind going next door to get Graham?"

"Graham Weaver? Why do you need him?"

"Because he's my best friend in the world."

"And here I thought your best friend was me," Lucy teased. "I came all the way here from Michigan, don't you know."

As Lucy had hoped, Mattie chuckled. "And I'll never forget your journey, neither. But I'd still be grateful if you went and got Graham for me."

Lucy was just going to warn Mattie that her request was foolish. That all Graham could do was everything Lucy could—but then Mattie spoke again, her voice wistful and sweet. "Graham will sit with me for hours."

"I can sit with you, Mattie—"

"I know. It's just, he's a *gut* friend." After a ragged breath, Mattie looked Lucy in the eye. "Even if you don't understand why I want him, would you still go see if he can stop by?"

Lucy got to her feet. "Of course. I'll go now." Leaning closer, she whispered, "But be warned. I'm going to tell your mother that I'm leaving you alone."

A weak smile lit Mattie's face. "I am willing to even put up with an hour of constant questioning and chatter in order to see Graham. Oh, I hope he'll be able to come over."

"He will," Lucy promised. After everything that Mattie had done for her, Lucy was willing to do whatever it took to bring Graham back over.

Even taking the chance of seeing his brother Calvin again.

Chapter 16

Lucy's pulse was beating loud, and she found herself checking and double-checking the state of her clothing while she approached the Weaver farm.

And wouldn't you know it? Her palms were damp, too.

All were signs of one thing: She was near Calvin.

Oh, but this wouldn't do. She was no innocent young girl. She'd already trusted a man based on charm and good looks—and had regretted that decision almost immediately. Surely that experience had taught her something?

Anything?

Schooling her features, she marched up to their front door and knocked. All she needed to do was relay the message and be on her way.

That was all.

"Lucy? Hi."

"Hi." Oh . . . against her best intentions, she was becoming tongue-tied around him again.

Standing in the shadow of the doorway, Calvin Weaver looked exactly as wonderful and handsome as he had every time their paths had crossed. Today his shirt was dark blue and it brought out the color of his eyes. For a moment, Lucy's breath hitched as she was drawn again to his deep, almost mesmerizing voice.

His head tilted to one side. "Is there a reason you stopped by?"

Instead of standing and staring at him? With effort, she pushed herself back to reality. "Actually, I'm here for Mattie. She asked to see Graham. Is he here?"

His gaze clouded for a moment, then cleared with a new resolve in his eyes. "Graham? Oh, of course." He stepped forward, joining her on the front porch. "Is Mattie all right?"

"I'm afraid she's having a tough time of it today. She's feeling sick and achy and sad. All she wants at the moment is Graham's company. I'm hoping he'll oblige her."

"I know he'll drop everything if she needs him . . ."

Just imagining such a thing made Lucy turn wistful. Were there men like that? Men who put women's needs before their own?

Once again, their eyes met. Held too long. As if embarrassed, Calvin finally looked away and cleared his throat.

"Graham is in the barn," he said, pointing toward his left.

Following the direction of his hand, she prepared to step back and walk away. It didn't matter how she felt when she was around him, she had a duty to perform and that duty didn't include investigating her feelings toward Calvin. *"Danke."*

"Wait! I, uh . . . I was just heading that way. How about I take you there?"

"You have time?" Oh, but she was grasping at just about anything in order to spend time with him!

"Of course I do. Or I could just tell him to go see Mattie for you. Spare you the trouble."

Walking the fifty steps or so wouldn't be much trouble. But being in Calvin's company a little bit longer might be, Lucy knew. If she left right away, Lucy could return to that retreat she'd built for herself. There in that safe place she would pretend she was functioning just fine. That she didn't need other people to be happy. That she didn't need another man in her life to complicate things. There, everything was as it should be.

Was as she'd hoped it would be.

Lord knew, she'd just been writing about that in her diary!

But, sometime during the past year, Lucy knew she'd also started to trust herself again. Oh, she was far from the vivacious woman she'd been before marrying Paul. But maybe—just maybe—she wasn't quite as skittish as she used to be.

Maybe she wasn't as fearful of her emotions. Or as fearful of other men. "Lucy, are you all right?"

"I'm sorry, I was woolgathering. You know, if you could go speak to Graham for me, I would be most grateful. I need to get back to Mattie. I would hate for her to be alone much longer."

"Ah. I'll go tell Graham, then." But still he paused. Searching her face, looking for encouragement.

And, oh, she yearned to give him that—but it wouldn't be good for her. Nor was it what she should be concentrating on. *Keep your mind on your task, Lucy,* she cautioned herself. *That's what is important.*

"Please don't forget to tell him to hurry. I mean, if he can come at all."

"I won't forget."

When she raised a hand to tell him goodbye, he shook his head.

"The least I could do is walk you to your buggy."

"That's not necessary—"

"It's on the way, yes?"

"You're right. I . . . *Danke.*"

He closed the door behind him, and they set out, first walking under the few feet of covered porch before strolling out into the April sun.

Calvin smiled her way as they approached her buggy, parked in the shadows of the barn so the horse could stand in relative comfort. "So . . . are you settled in okay at your cousin's house?"

"I am. Well, as much as I can, I suppose. There's a lot to do . . ." Her voice trailed off.

"I imagine so."

"How is Katie? And how is your uncle doing here? Is he enjoying being back in Jacob's Crossing?"

Calvin chuckled. "Katie is as she always is—a handful. And my uncle, I believe he's settling in fine."

"He's happy to be back here on the farm?"

"Oh, he's not here. He's living in town, near the library." His eyes sparkling with amusement, he said, "He's living above a donut shop."

"Truly?"

"Yep. And he likes it . . . a lot, too! You should stop by there one day. Or I could even take you?"

"Yes, I will stop by soon," she murmured, doing her best to ignore his offer without being too rude.

"You know, Lucy . . . one day we should spend some time together. Talk to each other more."

"About what?"

"Oh, this and that." After a beat, he continued: "You know, it's occurred to me that we've never really talked too much about our pasts."

"There's not much to say," she said quickly.

His eyebrows rose. "Oh?"

Now she felt like a liar. And worse, there was something in his eyes that told her he knew more than he was letting on.

But maybe that was simply her imagination? "Well . . . I had best get back to Mattie."

"And I'll tell Graham to head over soon."

He smiled, and just like clockwork, Lucy felt his interest in her. And felt her body respond. When he smiled her way, his gaze was soft, almost like a caress.

A moment passed.

Looking just as startled as she felt, Calvin cleared his throat. "Well, now. I should probably be on my way. Lucy, I am glad that our paths crossed."

She'd been glad to see him, too. *Too* glad. "I'll tell Mattie that Graham will be over as soon as he can," she said, injecting a friendly, easy tone into her voice.

"Yes. Please do." He stepped backward. Resumed a more formal posture. "Goodbye, Lucy."

"Goodbye to you, Calvin," she murmured as she finally got back into her buggy and released the break.

Through the cloud of pain and dizziness, Mattie recognized Graham's cool hand and matter-of-fact personality. "Graham," she tried to say, but even to her own ears, it sounded much like a grunt.

"Mattie, only you would try to speak at a time like this," he muttered. "Now, sit still and lean back, would you? You need to settle your head and your stomach for a time."

With a frown his way, she leaned back against the hard rails of the rocking chair. But instead of finding comfort, she only felt the hard planes digging into her spine and shoulder blades. Even her bottom and thighs felt sore.

The nurse had talked about an increased sensitivity to her skin, but this was more than she'd ever imagined happening. With a wince, she shifted, but that only served to push the rocker back and for her to lose her balance.

And for the nausea to return.

"Oh, Graham, I am sorry I asked you to come over. I shouldn't have. I'm in quite a state today."

But instead of chiding her like he usually did, Graham crouched in front of her and clasped her hands, comforting them in his warm, capable ones. "I'm not sorry at all. Matter of fact, I can't think of anywhere I'd rather be. It's a *verra* bad day you're havin' today, ain't it?"

Raising her gaze, she met his own. "It is a bad day. But it is no worse than that. It's just that the medicine they've been putting in my veins has made me feel terrible."

"I don't recall you complaining about the other time you had the chemotherapy. You didn't get so sick, did you?"

Fighting through her nausea, she attempted to explain things. "*Nee.* But the nurses said that the medicine is like that. It's a cumulative thing. All of a sudden, my body will say that it has had enough of this poison."

He winced.

And she knew she'd been too blunt. "Graham, I'm sorry," she said again, hating how whiny she sounded. Hating that he was witnessing it.

And that it was all her fault. "I asked Lucy to go get you because you always seem to know what to say. You always seem to be able to shake me out of whatever doldrums I fall into, and to make things so much better."

"It's a wonderful quality of mine," he said modestly— though she caught the gleam of amusement in his eye. "But today, however, I'm afraid I don't seem to be doing a good job of it." Almost tenderly, he brushed a thumb against her knuckles. "Is my being here making it worse?"

"Not at all." She slumped. "But I don't seem to be able to shake things."

Straightening, Graham reached for both her hands. "On your feet now."

He wanted to go walking? What in the world had gotten into him? "Graham—I feel too bad to go for a walk . . ."

"Oh, but you are a stubborn woman, Mattie Lapp," he

blurted, his voice as hard as it ever was. "Just listen for once, now, will ya?"

"I will." But still, she felt as lost as ever. She'd asked him over to help her feel better. But so far, all he seemed to be doing was getting her riled up.

Finding the strength from somewhere, Mattie obediently stood. "There. Is this better?"

"Nee." He sighed as he wrapped one arm around her and then ever so gently guided her to the long couch near the room's pair of windows.

Then, to her surprise, he sat down and guided her down right next to him. Close enough so that their sides touched. "But this is better now, *jah?"*

Every bone and muscle in her body felt like it was on fire—and felt weak as well. It was as if her body couldn't hold her weight any longer.

Oh, for heaven's sakes! She was going to black out! Either collapse against the back of a couch in a terrible, horrible slump . . . or lose herself completely and faint. As her world spun, she clutched at his arms. "Graham, I don't know how to tell you this, but I think I'm—"

She had no more words as he sighed and rearranged her in his arms. Now she was leaning back against his very solid, very hard and muscular chest.

His support felt so good, but surely it wasn't appropriate. "Graham, maybe—"

"Shh, Mattie," he commanded. After a second, he spoke again, his voice smoother, almost like a song. "Hush, now, Mattie. I've got ya. Just relax now. Please, just rest."

Little by little, her body conformed to his. Slowly relaxing. At least her body was, because her mind was spinning. What they were doing certainly wasn't proper. No, she surely knew she wasn't supposed to be lying against him.

Alone. Once more, this was certainly not what she had intended to happen when she'd asked Graham to come over.

But as her muscles slowly relaxed and his calm heartbeat thudded a reassuring rhythm against her body, Mattie knew she didn't care anymore.

An overwhelming sense of relief and comfort floated through her, as the pain that had racked her body slowly ebbed and flowed into something manageable.

"I've got ya, Mattie," he said again, rubbing one calloused hand along her arm. "I'm glad ya sent for me, and I promise you this—there's nowhere else I need to be. Nowhere else I'd *rather* be."

"I'm glad we're friends," she murmured, feeling sleep start to tug at her.

Behind her, she felt his body tense for a moment, like he was hiding a kind of secret pain. "I . . . I am, too, Mattie. I'm *verra* glad we're friends as well." He coughed. "Now, though . . . it is time for you to stop this nonsense of fighting, and let your body relax. Take a nap, why don't you? It's what your body needs."

As if on cue, her eyelids did seem heavy—too heavy to try to keep open. "You won't go?"

"I won't go anywhere at all. Not until you wake up. Sleep, Mattie," he repeated. His words sounded sweet, but held a hint of iron will. "Sleep and dream sweet dreams."

There was his bossy attitude. And the curious way he had of telling her what to do . . .

It was so familiar, and so right.

And that is what she thought about as she closed her eyes and finally followed directions. There, in Graham's arms.

The only place that made her feel safe.

Chapter 17

The library was cool. That was about the nicest compliment you could say about it. A remodeled old house, its rooms were small, the ceiling was low, and a musty smell permeated every room.

John didn't know if that was from the books or the building. Either way, he wasn't a fan of it. Of course, that wasn't why he'd come to the library, anyway. Not really. He had promised Katie he'd pick up some picture books for her. But his niece wasn't the reason he'd been looking forward to visiting the building. He'd come to see her.

"Couldn't stay away, could you, John?" Jayne Donovan said as she watched him walk toward the circulation desk.

"I had some extra time, and so I thought I'd check things out." He swallowed. "And I promised my five-year-old niece that I'd pick up some picture books for her. Could you help me with that?"

"I can." And with a smile to her somewhat heavyset partner, Jayne circled the desk and stood in front of him. "But first, how about a tour?"

He was not going to notice her legs in that slim-fitting navy skirt. "I'd like that. If you have time."

She started walking, but had the audacity of looking back at him over her shoulder. Obviously, to see if he'd follow.

And he did. Actually, he followed her like a lamb.

"Lucy, go take a break," Aunt Jenna said late Monday afternoon. They'd spent the last hour changing Mattie's sheets, washing the bathroom, and making bread. No longer was there a cool breeze, the last remnants of winter lingering in the air. No, suddenly, it was muggy and warm. Inside, the house felt humid and hot, and Lucy had found herself wiping her brow every few minutes.

As Jenna sipped her glass of water, she looked ready for a rest. "I'm going to sit down for a few moments and cool off. Mattie's already fallen asleep on the wicker couch on the back porch. Why don't you go take some time for yourself?"

Lucy didn't even know what she'd do. Stalwartly, she said, "I didn't come here to find time for myself. I came to help."

"And you have, child." After another sip of water, she set the glass down. "However, even the best of caregivers cannot give all that they have of themselves. If you do, there will be nothing left for Mattie when she needs it. I promise you that." Stepping forward, Aunt Jenna casually wrapped an arm around Lucy's shoulders and directed her toward the front door. "Now, I don't mean to sound ungrateful, but what I'd really like for you to do is to leave here for a few hours."

"Come now, Aunt Jenna—"

"I mean it. If you're here, you will be thinking about Mattie or about the cooking or the cleaning." The corners of Jenna's eyes crinkled. "And if you do that, I will feel obligated to cook and clean, too."

"But—"

"How about a walk? I think it's far cooler outside than in here . . ." She smiled, nodding. "Yes, that's what you should do. Go for a walk. That's the best way to clear your head."

Lucy was tempted to argue the point, but she had a sneaking suspicion that her aunt was right. Paul's criticism and hurtful words had been clanging in her head, reminding her of her faults.

And at the moment, each flaw in her personality felt huge. Too big. Making her feel disappointed in herself. Mattie was still struggling, both physically and emotionally. Despite Lucy's very best efforts, her cousin didn't seem to have improved much at all.

Making Lucy feel like the worst sort of failure. She needed to escape the work and her inner demons and do her best to feel rejuvenated.

Perhaps a walk was exactly what she needed. "Is there a good walking path nearby?"

"As a matter of fact, there is. Beyond the barn, you'll see

a thicket of honeysuckle. Right behind that, you will find a worn trail. Go ahead and take that. It winds through the woods and even goes near a creek. It's wonderful-*gut*."

Lucy was slightly suspicious of her aunt's eager advice, but she knew it would be useless to refuse. The day was beautiful, too beautiful to think about hitching up a buggy and driving in unfamiliar places.

No, she'd rather be out in the fresh air getting some exercise.

"All right. I'll go for a walk. But I won't be too long."

"You take all the time you want, dear Lucy." After a pause, she murmured, "I promise you, not much will have changed before you get back."

There was a hint of desperation in her aunt's voice. "Aunt Jenna? Is there more going on with Mattie's health than I realized? Did you get news from the doctor?"

"No. It is just the same as it ever was." Visibly trying to be upbeat, Jenna pointed to the door. "Now, we've spoken of this enough. Go now, and enjoy your afternoon. Oh! I just thought of something. Take this pail. Over near the creek, you'll see a patch of blackberries. For some reason, they're ripe early this year. Why don't you pick some for us? Mattie always enjoys blackberry cobbler."

Basket in hand, Lucy soon left the shadowed darkness of the house and walked into the open sunshine, with the goal of gathering blackberries—and clearing her head.

She wasn't sure if she could do the latter easily, but she hugged the given task to her heart. She'd picked enough blackberries over the years to know that it would not be difficult.

The path underfoot was rocky and a bit jagged. The grass had the look of giving up its effort to grow under the many feet that tromped over it.

It was no trouble to find the glorious yellow and white honeysuckle flowers. All she had to do was follow their sweet scent.

And, as Jenna had told her, a well-worn path lay just beyond the flowering vines. Feeling a bit like an adventurer, Lucy swung her metal pail as she followed the trail.

First, the path meandered in between two freshly planted fields. The dirt there was dark and full of nutrients—and manure. Its smell overpowered the light floral scent with a vengeance. Wrinkling her nose, Lucy continued on, half looking for men plowing the fields behind teams of horses. But no one was around.

She was alone in the silence.

Little by little, Lucy felt the muscles in her shoulders relax.

Yes, it was probably a very good thing that she was taking some time to herself. Paul had been coming to her dreams almost every night, berating her, hurting her. She'd awoken just this morning with him twisting her arm, pulling her toward him. It had taken a good five minutes for her breathing to slow and reality to return.

To remind herself that he was gone. That he would never hurt her again.

Every day with him had been full of ups and downs. Uncertainty had ruled her life. She hadn't known who to turn to for help, especially since no one in her community had wanted to acknowledge that she was suffering at Paul's hand.

Lucy stopped for a moment, prepared to push the painful reminders away, but then decided to let them fill her head. She was alone now, and no one was around to witness her disappointment or her complete sense of helplessness.

And, well, perhaps it was better to think of these things every so often? Maybe then they wouldn't ravage her dreams and turn peaceful slumber into nightmares.

She recalled one time when she and Paul were at church. After the service, he overheard some of her friends teasing her about their childless state. Far from being cruel, they'd been teasing her about her extra free time, since she wasn't nursing babies and changing diapers all day long.

Though she'd wished her life had been different, Lucy had smiled. She'd yearned for a babe, too, but knew that was in God's hands.

But when Paul heard the other women and had caught sight of her smile, his dark look told everyone present that he didn't share their amusement with her "easy" life.

He'd stopped. "Yes, Lucy is a disappointment, to be sure," he'd said coldly. "I would've never married her if I had imagined that she was barren."

Everyone present had been shocked. Then her friend Marta had dared to look Paul over and mock him. "It takes two, you know," she quipped before Lucy could stop her. "You don't know it is Lucy's fault. Maybe the problem lies with you?"

The girls had giggled.

And Lucy's spirits had plummeted as Paul's expression turned thunderous. "Lucy, you will meet me by our buggy in four minutes."

Marta and the others had stared at her husband, wide-eyed. "But Lucy was going to eat lunch with us!" Krista protested. "Surely you wouldn't make her leave right now?"

Silently Lucy had tried to stop the girls from saying another word. The damage had been done—nothing was going to make Paul's temper cool. Putting him off would only make things worse.

But instead of falling silent, other girls had joined in. "You'll have to take her home later, Paul. We were going to talk about plans for a charity quilt we're going to be stitching."

"And we haven't seen her in ages," another added.

Paul cleared his throat, a sure sign that he was holding in his temper. Barely.

Because she didn't want to upset the girls, or embarrass herself any further, Lucy stood. Tried to smile. "It's all right. Really, it is. I'll be ready in four minutes, Paul," she'd said, her voice hardly shaking at all. "I promise I will."

"See that you will be."

Marta hadn't wanted to give up, though. "But, Paul, what about lunch?"

"She can cook our lunch at home." Eyes frosty, he turned her way. "Do you understand, Lucy?"

"Of course."

The other girls had gathered around her as soon as Paul marched off. Marta had been terribly contrite. "I'm so sorry, Lucy. I never would have been so bold if I'd thought Paul really was so sensitive about your childless state. After all, it's only been a year." With a comforting smile, she'd patted her arm. "Before you know it, you'll have a *boppli* on the way."

Lucy had done her best to act as if she believed Marta. She'd shaken her head and tried to pretend that she wasn't disappointed. Or afraid of being alone with Paul.

But there was nothing she could do. Paul was her husband, and she'd wanted to marry him. It didn't matter if he turned out to be nothing like the man she'd fallen for.

No, all that really mattered was that she couldn't get away from him. She was his wife now. For better or worse.

And that day, when they'd gotten home, it had been one of the worst, indeed.

"Lucy? Is that you?"

Startled from her memories, Lucy turned and blinked. And then, there he was—the man so different from her current nightmares. "Calvin," she murmured, taking in his dark pants and cornflower blue shirt. The black suspenders and his straw hat. His smooth, tan cheeks, and the bump in the line of his nose.

And suddenly, her head cleared of old memories. "Hi. I mean, hello."

"Hello, to you, too." Moving closer, he looked her over. "I never expected to see you here."

With relief, she pushed the rest of her memories away. "I'm looking for a blackberry patch. What about you?"

"Oh, my brothers and I like using this trail. We take it when we don't feel like hitching up the buggy." Eyes sparkling, he added, "This path links our two houses, did you know that?"

"I didn't."

"Well, you'll see Graham on it more often than not. He does enjoy visiting Mattie, you know."

"He can't seem to stay away." Feeling vaguely conspicuous, Lucy swung her pail. "Well. I had best go pick berries. I promised my aunt that I would."

"A useful project."

They were standing close now. Lucy noticed faint dark flecks in the blue of his eyes. Noticed a scar near his eyebrow. And suddenly, the last thing in the world she wanted was peace and quiet and more time to dwell on the past. "Care to walk with me?" she asked. "Or do you need to go on your way?"

"I'll accompany you, for sure." For a few minutes they walked along the path, the thicket of vines growing heavy on their left, tall oaks and maples reaching to the heavens on their right.

"It's lovely here. A true blessing."

"It is." Looking at her sideways, he murmured, "Lucy, forgive me if I'm being too personal, but when I came upon you, you looked mighty upset. As if you had far more on your mind than mere berries." He looked her way, his eyes calmly searching. "Are you all right?"

"Of course." But even she knew she'd blurted that too quickly.

"No. I don't think so." Looking at her more carefully, he said, "Though the pain I first glimpsed in your eyes has faded, you still look near tears."

She didn't dare tell him a lie, she was too shaken up inside to focus on one for long. "Actually, I was upset, but I'm better now. I was just spending a bit too much time worrying about things I cannot fix."

"Like Mattie?"

His question embarrassed her. Yes, she was worried about Mattie's health of course. But that wasn't what had occupied her mind. "Like Mattie. And worrying about some things from my past."

They walked for a bit while Calvin seemed to consider that. Finally, he looked her way again. "It's been my experience that the past is easier if you come to terms with it and move on."

"It's not that easy," she snapped, then instantly regretted her words.

But instead of getting mad, Calvin merely laughed. "You're right about that. But moving on is a useful goal, I think."

Charmed by his words as much as his laughter, Lucy nodded.

As a robin flew by, and they stood and watched her land in her nest, a new peace settled between them. Feeling as comforting as the breeze on their cheeks. After another moment, Calvin looked her over from head to toe. "This worry that seems to have gripped you . . . it isn't about Mattie, is it?"

"No. I was just thinking about some memories that I usually try hard to ignore. Usually I only dream about my past; but today, for some reason, memories decided to spring forward while I'm awake." Recalling how defeated she'd felt before Calvin had appeared, she added, "With a vengeance."

They were in front of the blackberry bushes. The air surrounding them was full of the berries' sweet, fruit-ripe scent—and it sweetened her mood as well. She felt so different with Calvin.

Almost as if she wasn't as damaged as she imagined she was.

Without a word, he took the tin pail from her hand. Then, with great care, he pulled a berry from the branch closest and just as easily dropped the succulent-looking fruit into the pail. "One," he said with a smile.

Next to him, she plucked another berry and deposited it in the pail as well. "Two," she said with a smile of her own.

"Sometimes when we don't know what to do about the past, we have to concentrate on the present," he said quietly. "I've found that to be enough."

"I, too, have found that to be enough," she said, pulling off another pair of berries and tossing them into the pail.

Over and over, they repeated the motions. Together, as the sun fell on their shoulders and the warm fruit stained their fingers, they worked on the task. Every so often a bee would buzz by, angry at their intrusion to its private world.

Calvin would carefully wave it away with a brush of his hand and then smile at her as they both sighed in relief that yet again, they hadn't gotten stung.

The pail got heavy enough for Calvin to set it on the ground. Eager to fill it to the brim, Lucy knelt in front of the bushes, reaching into the thorny branches for more fruit.

And then got stung. "Ow!" she yelped, jerking her hand back in surprise.

With two movements, he clasped her injured hand in between his own. "Lucy?"

"The bees finally got the best of me." She tried to laugh off the sting, but couldn't quite succeed.

Gently, he turned her hand in his, rubbed his thumbs over the bottom of her palm, tentatively searching for her injury. Lucy turned her hand to show him the red mark on the end of her thumb. "It is nothing."

"It is something." Carefully, he inspected her tiny hurt. "It doesn't look like the stinger is there."

She pressed her thumb against his hand, trying to see how much pressure she could place on it. "I don't think it's there, either." When he still looked at her thumb with a frown, she smiled. "Calvin, don't look so worried. It's just a sting, *jah*? And it's my own fault. The bee didn't care for me invading his home."

"I fear you are right about that." Her hand still clasped between his two, she watched him raise it slightly. Almost to his lips.

Her breath hitched, startling them both.

Looking perturbed, he dropped his hands.

Lucy felt his absence immediately—even deep inside her. In the place she wished was filled with more than just bad memories and aches.

When Calvin looked her way again, his expression was bare and honest. "Lucy, what thoughts have claimed you so completely? What is it that you wish you didn't remember?"

Her mouth went dry as she stared. A full minute passed, but Calvin didn't push. Instead, he merely stood right next to her. Waiting.

And so she took a chance. "I wish that I could forget about my husband," she whispered.

"Ah," he said quietly.

Lucy noticed he didn't seem all that surprised. "He passed away."

If anything, Calvin looked even more worried. "Lucy . . . how did he die?"

"He fell from a ladder and broke his neck."

He swallowed. "Was he . . . was that Paul?"

She nodded, then stared at him in confusion. "How did you know his name?"

A second passed. Two. Finally he lifted his chin. "I, um. I read about him."

What he said made no sense. "Read? What are you talking about?"

"I . . . I saw his name in your diary, Lucy." While her world shifted and dimmed, he continued. "On the train, I found your journal. I was going to give it right back to you—"

He'd *found* her journal? He'd *read* it?

He knew?

"B-but you didn't," she said—well, *stuttered*. Pure shame and embarrassment coursed through her as she remembered some of the things she'd written. Some of the awful, awful things she'd written. The anger and hurt and relief she'd felt. Not a bit of it meant for another person to see.

"We argued, and I was afraid you wouldn't understand that I had just been trying to be helpful." The skin around his lips paled, showing how hard he was striving for control. "So I decided to give the journal to you here in Jacob's Crossing."

"But you haven't."

"Things were going better. And I was confused. The words I read in your diary, they didn't seem to go with the woman I knew."

Despair sank in. *The words he'd read.* Doing her best to reclaim her voice, Lucy said, "So you read my diary. Without asking. Calvin, when were you planning to give it back?"

He raised his hands in surrender. "I know what I did was wrong. I shouldn't have opened the book. Once I knew what you'd written . . . I shouldn't have read a word."

"But you did." She shook her head. "Calvin, I can't believe it. I almost trusted you. I almost thought you were different."

"Different from Paul?" Stepping forward, he reached for her hand. She yanked her fingers away, but he tightened his grip. Forcing her to stay next to him. To listen to him. "Lucy, why did you want him dead? That's such a sin. Your hate, your anger . . . it's stunning. Why?"

As his words hit her hard, an almost eerie feeling of calm filled her soul. All of a sudden, telling him the truth didn't seem so hard. "Because he beat me, Calvin. Because every single day that I lived with him, I lived in fear." She shook her head. "Because in so many ways, he took everything I had to give, and twisted it. Made me feel unworthy. Dirty."

Tears entered his eyes as his grip relaxed. Dropped her hand. "Lucy, I don't know what to say. I'm so—"

"Don't say it, Calvin. Whatever you do . . . don't say another word to me ever again."

And then, like a child, she ran.

Ran back the way she came, along the windy, uneven trail. Alone, toward Mattie, and to her past.

And realized too late that she'd left her aunt's pail on the ground at Calvin's feet. Filled to the brim with ripe blackberries, warm from the sun.

Chapter 18

Calvin let her go. Of course, he didn't think he would've been able to follow Lucy even if he'd been of the mind to. His feet felt planted to the ground, stunned by what had just happened.

She now knew he'd kept her diary.

No, it was more than that, he pushed himself to admit. She now knew he'd *read* her diary—because he'd told her in the clumsiest way imaginable.

Mind spinning, Calvin watched her pale gray dress fade into the distance as she scrambled through the path. Within seconds, she disappeared behind the Scotch pine that had sprung up years ago.

Then, she was gone, leaving only her pail of berries, the faint fragrance of her soap, and the startling words they exchanged hanging steadfastly to his consciousness.

Lucy had been married, and Paul had been her husband.

Little by little, confusion of what was right and wrong spun together in his mind. Calvin forced himself to come to terms with what he now knew. Her husband had hurt her. Hurt her a lot.

Oh, he should just call it what it was, he chided himself. Lucy's husband had abused her. That was why she'd been so angry in her diary. That was why she'd been relieved at his death.

Taking a seat on the hard ground, he leaned back against an old wooden post. Then he tried to remember what, exactly, she'd written in her journal. But for the life of him, none of it was terribly clear. Perhaps he'd been too stunned by her sentiment to recall it all.

Or perhaps he'd felt too guilty—both by what he was doing and by his feelings for Lucy.

In his world, wedding vows were sacred. People didn't divorce, and they accepted the good with the bad in the marriage. As another bee hovered nearby, Calvin wondered just how bad Lucy's marriage had been.

And he wondered how scarred she was from such a life. Would she ever be able to love again? To marry again?

Just as soon as they came, Calvin tried to shake off such musings. His thoughts were shameful, that's what they were. It would be far better to concentrate on his own feelings instead of Lucy's. As he looked at the pail she'd abandoned, filled to the brim with berries, Calvin stretched out his legs, uneager to return home until he had a handle on his emotions.

Until he had a plan of what to do next. Of course, what

could he do besides apologize to Lucy again for not immediately returning her book? But what then? Would there ever be anything more after that?

The afternoon sun beat down on his shoulders and face. He closed his eyes and let the sun warm his skin. And let himself think about her some more. Lucy was such a tiny thing. All golden hair, pale, creamy cheeks, and light brown eyes. So watchful, so full of secrets. Hesitant.

But also strong, too. In many ways, she was the exact opposite of Gwen, who'd gotten bored with their relationship and had moved on, her chin held high. She'd had no regrets about how she'd embarrassed him, or how she'd changed her mind so suddenly.

Yes, Lucy was strong. Strong enough for him to ask her more questions. And perhaps ask if she feared him.

Suddenly, he knew that he wanted to be there for her, at least as a friend, as someone she could trust. But perhaps as something more, too.

Slowly, Calvin got to his feet and grasped the pail. Later he would carry it to the Lapps'. Perhaps tomorrow, or even the next day. But until then, he knew they both needed time. He needed to process her revelation and she needed time to deal with his confession and her own emotions.

And if they had that time, perhaps when he asked her if she feared him, Lucy would be able to tell the truth.

And he would be able to accept it.

"Are you picking berries in your spare time now, Calvin?" Loyal asked when Calvin entered the kitchen.

Ignoring his brother's sarcasm, Calvin shook his head. "The berries are Lucy's. She forgot them at the patch. I'll give them to her later."

Loyal grinned. "Ah."

Calvin glared. "What do you mean by that?"

"I mean that I knew you fancied her. You carrying her pail of berries proves that."

Honestly. How come younger brothers could still be irritating, even at twenty-four? "I don't see how this pail proves anything."

"It proves that for some reason the two of you ended up picking fruit together this fine afternoon . . . and then got so distracted that somehow Lucy managed to forget her fruit."

They certainly had gotten distracted. But that wasn't something Loyal needed to know. "I think your mind's gone missing. Maybe you've been out in the sun too long."

Loyal grinned wider. "Care to tell me how you just 'happened' to meet Lucy on your walk?"

Oh, this was too much. He did not care to say another word about his walk, or his conversation with Lucy. Actually, he didn't seem to be able to think about anything other than what she'd told him. "No."

Loyal's playful attitude stilled. "Calvin? Are you all right? Did something happen?"

For a moment, Calvin ached to tell his brother about what he'd discovered about Lucy. And about what he'd done. But it was too embarrassing to have to admit that he'd done something as juvenile as reading a woman's private diary. Something so wrong.

And, well, Lucy's past was hers to tell, not his.

"Something happened, but it's a long story."

"I have time." He pointed to one of the kitchen chairs. "Why don't we talk?"

"Thank you for the offer, but I can't talk about her. Our conversation was private, anyway. I can't betray a confidence."

Whether it was his words, or the serious way he said them, Loyal backed down. "All right, then. I understand."

Now that his brother wasn't ribbing him so much, Calvin finally took the time to truly look at what his brother was doing—reading the *Budget*, the Amish newspaper. Beside the newspaper were a bankbook and several legal-looking documents. "What are you doing?"

Now it was Loyal's turn to be secretive. "Oh, nothing much. Just doing some research."

"Research for what?" Taking a seat beside him, Calvin edged the paper closer. Scanning the open page, he saw nothing of interest . . . besides an ad for a land auction. Slowly, Calvin met his brother's gaze.

After a pause, Loyal cleared his throat. "I've heard some rumors about the Hostetler land going up for auction. This ad proves the rumors are true."

Calvin knew the family his brother spoke of. "Did Ella's mother finally pass?"

Loyal nodded. "She did, soon after you and Katie left. Then I heard rumors that she's not going to wait long to put her land up for sale. I suppose she's ready to move on."

Calvin felt sorry for Ella. He wasn't particularly close to either Ella Hostetler or her mother, but he'd known

Mrs. Hostetler had been suffering from some kind of kidney disease for some time. "I'm sorry I missed the service."

"It was a quiet funeral, as you might expect."

"I imagine Ella would have preferred it that way, her being an only child and all."

A line formed between Loyal's brows. "I think she did. Both she and her mother have already suffered so much, you know."

"I heard she's been bedridden for the last six months, with only Ella to care for her."

"That's a heavy burden. A terribly heavy burden." Loyal frowned. "From the looks of things, her mother's illness took its toll on Ella—and on their finances."

Directing his attention back to the paper, Calvin pointed. "She's already putting the farm up for sale?"

"Uh-huh. Word is that Ella is suffering both from her mother's loss . . . and from financial worries. He heard that Ella was interviewing for a job at the library. And that she was looking at apartments in town."

Calvin whistled low. "That's a shame for her. Their land is wonderful-*gut*. It has both woods and a creek."

"It does, indeed." His brother cleared his throat. "Though I feel sorry for Ella, I am enough of a realist to know that someone is going to get that land." He paused, looking squarely at Calvin, his jaw set. "I want it."

"But I'm not sure if we have a need for more farmland, Loyal."

"Not for 'we,' for me."

Stunned, Calvin stared at his brother. "Why do you

need your own bit of land? It seems to me that we have more than our fair share between the three of us."

"I'm just looking ahead. One day you're going to marry—and, eventually, you'll want the property to pass on to your sons."

Marry? Sons? Loyal always had been the type to look ten steps ahead instead of just one. "Don'tcha think you're rushin' things a bit? I'm not courting Gwen anymore, you know. I don't think we'll be needin' to worry about the future of our farmland for quite some time."

"I know we've got some time," Loyal retorted. "And, Calvin, I'm sorry to be blunt, but the truth is, I'm glad Gwen is out of your life. She was no good for you."

"I realize that now. Going away to Uncle John's was the right decision."

"Maybe it was in more ways than one? You being there brought John back to us. And then, of course, you met Lucy."

Before Calvin could comment, Loyal stacked the papers spread out in front of him into a nice neat pile. "I need to move on with my life, too, brother. One day you will marry. Graham, too. And I have no desire to all live together in this house."

"Well, of course not—"

"Then, you understand why I'm looking at this Hostetler property. I'm just thinking ahead. And I do have my money, you know."

Calvin didn't even like the reminder. Five years ago when their father passed away, they'd been shocked to learn that their father had left them each some funds, in addition to leaving their mother with enough money to live independently for the rest of her life.

Calvin had been too numb with grief to do much but follow the banker's advice and open up a savings account where the funds would be safe and accrue some interest until the time came that he'd need it.

But obviously Loyal had been thinking about his future more in terms of what he wanted instead of what he didn't have.

For the last few years, Calvin had grown and lived his life, but his heart and mind had been firmly planted on what he'd lost.

He'd mourned his father's death and struggled to keep his family's routine the same. He'd struggled to fill the void his father left, doing his best to be more than just an older brother to Loyal and Graham. And, of course, he'd done his best to be a father figure for Katie.

However, though many things were the same as they'd ever been, they weren't really the same. Not at all.

And, he realized with dismay, he'd done the same thing with Gwen. He'd not been sure about the two of them. But instead of telling her how he felt, he'd turned introspective. Pensive.

Which she had seen as a rejection.

Even when Gwen had moved on to Will, he had still clung to her letter, memorizing each word, dwelling on things that could not be changed.

"I . . . I am glad for you, Loyal," he finally said, even

holding out his hand to prove it. "If you win the Hostetler land in auction, it will be a wonderful-*gut* thing for you, and for our family."

Relief filled his brother's eyes. "It makes me *verra* happy to hear you say that, Calvin. I didn't want to do this behind your back."

"I will always believe in you. Don't ever feel like you can't speak to me about anything."

"Calvin?"

"Yes?"

"I feel the same way about you, you know. I'm always here if you need to talk. Brothers are more than strong arms and backs, ain't so? We can also help each other . . ." And with that, his brother left, leaving Calvin to ponder his brother's words . . . and realize they were true.

After setting the berries in the sink, Calvin turned the faucet on cold and splashed a handful of water over his flushed cheeks.

Chapter 19

Paul's neck hung limply to one side. After touching his skin, Lucy backed up. As her thick-soled boots scuffed the floor, dust flew into her face. Her eyes teared up.

Next to her, Star whined his displeasure.

After an eternity passed, Lucy reached out and pet the dog's ears. "I know," she murmured. "This . . . this is a scary thing. Ain't so?"

In a daze, Lucy slowly turned. Walked to their horse's stall. With mechanical movements, she brought Blaze to the buggy and hitched him up.

Then, with Paul still staring up at her blankly, she turned and called for Star. One leap brought Star onto the leather seat, his tongue hanging out in anticipation. "Gut hund," she murmured.

Paul never let the dog ride in the buggy. Not ever.

As she motioned Blaze forward, Lucy realized things had already changed. Paul couldn't tell her "No" anymore.

It was a relatively short distance to the bishop's home. There, she would tell him about the accident, and rely on him to tell her what to do.

The street was empty. Blaze's clip-clopping echoed through the still evening air.

When she was halfway to the bishop's home, the tears began to fall. One by one, they splashed against her cheeks, fell onto her lap. Next to her, Star whined and cuddled closer.

The dog's comfort spurred her crying. Lucy's shoulders jerked, shook.

And when she appeared at Bishop Lund's door, and told him about Paul, his wife had enfolded her into a gentle hug.

"Ach, Lucy. I am so sorry. It is a terrible thing, this."

That's when Lucy knew she'd never tell a soul that her tears were ones of relief. No one needed to know that. Not ever.

Gasping for air, her eyes opened wide.

Calvin now knew, too.

As she sat in bed and welcomed the morning sun, Lucy fought back the fears that seemed to constantly plague her. And remembered how hurt and confused and, well . . . angry she'd been for months after Paul had died.

Knowing her feelings were shameful, she'd poured all her secrets into the journal. And now Calvin had read them.

How could she ever face Calvin again? Every time she remembered the things she'd written—and Calvin's expression when he told her that she'd sinned—she flinched.

Just as if he'd attacked her physically.

Just as Paul had.

She shifted in the bed, carefully rearranging the sheets around her body. Reviewing the whole conversation with Calvin once again.

She closed her eyes and winced as she realized the crux of it all—he still had the journal! She'd been such a fool to trust him. So silly to ever imagine any man could push his own feelings aside and care enough to try to see her point of view.

Still gripped by demons, she was startled by the footsteps outside her door. Brought back to reality.

Ah, yes. It was time to push her own concerns to the back of her mind and try to concentrate on her cousin. Tomorrow, she and Mattie would be going back to the hospital for another chemotherapy treatment, which would begin another bout of nausea and discomfort. The cycle was grueling. With each day, her admiration for Mattie grew. Without a doubt, she was one of the strongest women she'd ever had the good fortune to know.

That's what she needed to concentrate on. Slowly, she got out of bed and prepared to shower. Anything instead of dwelling on what couldn't be changed.

Thirty minutes later, Lucy forced a smile to her lips as she walked into Mattie's bedroom. "How about some breakfast?"

"Not right now."

Though Mattie was out of bed and sitting curled up in a chair, to Lucy's eyes, her cousin looked as despondent as ever. "Hot tea, perhaps?"

"No." As if realizing her tone was rude, she softened her voice. "Maybe in a little bit?"

Lucy bit her lip in frustration. She'd been hoping Mattie would be able to eat well today, since there was little doubt that she wouldn't be able to stomach much over the next few days. "All right. If you're sure you'll try to eat something soon?"

"Sure. Just don't push so."

Her cousin didn't like to be treated as if she had no choices. Since Lucy could understand that, she was doing her best to give Mattie as many options as possible for how to spend her days. That way Mattie would be able to have at least a little control over her life.

"What would you like to do this morning?"

Mattie pursed her lips. "Well, the weather is lovely, to be sure. Maybe we could go for a walk?"

"A walk would be *gut* for both of us," she said agreeably. "As long as you eat something first." Before Mattie could protest again, she looped her arm through her cousin's and playfully guided her into the kitchen.

"You weren't going to give up until you got your way, were you?" Mattie asked, her tone wry.

Lucy decided to let that quip pass as she opened the refrigerator. "Oh, look. Your *mamm* made some granola this morning; and there're apples and oranges, too. I think some oatmeal or toast and jam would taste very fine with that, don'tcha think?"

"I suppose." Mattie sat in her wooden chair, leaned back, and watched Lucy bustle around the kitchen. "If you really think we should eat now."

"I do."

Mattie said nothing. Instead, she crossed her arms on the table and rested her elbows on the worn wooden surface. She stayed silent, though Lucy wasn't sure if it was because she was miffed or only seeking a respite from the effort of making conversation.

So much seemed to affect her these days.

After Lucy had set the water to boiling on the stove for the oatmeal, she noticed Mattie looking a little bit interested.

She sipped her hot tea when Lucy brought it to her, and smiled when Lucy placed on the table two bowls of oatmeal and glasses filled with granola, fruit, and yogurt. "Perhaps I was a little bit hungry," she said. After a brief, quiet prayer, she dug in. After two bites, she looked at Lucy in surprise. "This tastes wonderful-*gut*."

"I think so, too."

When they were almost finished, Mattie put her spoon down. "So, what happened the other day on your walk?"

Lucy's stomach sank. This was exactly what she was hoping *not* to think about! "Nothing."

"Come now. You left for your walk with an empty pail. Since the weather was so nice, neither Mamm nor I expected to see you for an hour or two. But you came home after little more than an hour . . . crying."

"I know. "

"What happened? Please tell me. Instead of coming home with a pail of blackberries and a lighter heart, you returned with only a terribly sad expression." She leaned forward. "Come now. All I do is sit in bed all day. At the very least, tell me what happened to the pail?" Looking almost like her former self, Mattie's eyes sparkled. "Let's see . . . you were besieged by a hungry bear?"

"Of course not."

"Raccoon?"

"Oh, Mattie."

"I'm waiting . . ."

"All right. I left it at the patch," she said quickly. "I must have forgotten it when I left."

"You forgot it after picking berries?" Mattie's expression told Lucy that she didn't buy that excuse for a second.

And Lucy didn't really blame her. "Um, leaving it on the ground was just a mistake. And simply a small one, too. Mattie, there's no need for you to be so worried. I promise I'll go fetch it later today."

"It is not the pail nor the berries I am thinking of." Mattie looked her up and down like she was a recalcitrant child at school. "Lucy," she said with exaggerated patience. "I know you saw Calvin on your walk. Mamm told me."

Alarm, and a bit of irritation, coursed through Lucy. Had her Aunt Jenna really been keeping tabs on her? And was it really her aunt's business whom she talked to, anyway? "How did she know I saw him?"

Mattie pushed her chair back and stood up, then gathered her dishes and walked to the sink. "So, your secret is out," she said airily as she turned on the faucet.

Indeed it was. Lucy scrambled to meet her at the sink. "I've got this. Why don't you sit for a bit?"

"I can wash dishes, Lucy. I get tired of sitting and watching."

Too flustered to argue, Lucy gave in. "All right." After squirting dish soap into the sink, she began scrubbing bowls after Mattie scraped them off. The warm, soapy water helped calm her frazzled nerves.

When Mattie looked at her again, her eyes full of concern, Lucy knew it was time to lean on her cousin. Mattie wanted to be thought of as more than just a cancer patient—and Lucy desperately needed someone to confide in. "You're right. I did see Calvin. And . . . something happened between us." With a deep breath, she said, "Calvin found my diary on the train and kept it."

Mattie stilled. "And?"

"And Calvin read some truly hateful things that I wrote about Paul."

"He shouldn't have read a word."

"I know." Her body relaxed. Oh, it felt good to share her anger and dismay with her cousin! "He was, um . . . horrified about what I wrote on the pages."

"*He* was horrified by *your* feelings?" Mattie shook her head. "If he could have seen you. Even once." Her eyes burned bright. "Lucy, do you remember your broken arm? Your black eye? Your . . . your bruises?"

"Of course." Of course, she remembered so much more. "Calm down. *Jah*—of course I remember." Though she couldn't believe she was defending Calvin, she still did. "But Calvin wasn't there. He didn't know . . ." Lucy stumbled, trying to verbalize all her feelings, yet trying to put it all behind her, too. "Calvin really doesn't realize how it was."

"Well, I'll tell him. I'll be happy to help him understand how difficult your life was."

"You'll do no such thing. Besides, I did tell him a little . . ."

"Good. So, how did you end things?"

Lucy ducked her head. "I ran away."

To her surprise, Mattie chuckled. "Oh, Lucy. You poor dear. Ach. Well, don't worry about the journal or Calvin. Things will get better."

Lucy glanced at her in surprise. "You sound so sure."

Dipping her hands in the soapy water once again, Mattie handed her a spoon. "I am. See, sometimes I wonder if our two situations aren't all that different."

Drying that spoon, she asked, "What do you mean?"

"Well, something happened to me that I didn't expect— and it's taken just about all my energy to fight it. Perhaps not all that different from your life with Paul."

"Paul's behavior was a slow progression, Mattie. I saw the signs. My problem was that I didn't act on it quickly enough." Though, Lucy realized, there wasn't anything she could do. She'd been trapped.

Mattie handed her a glass. "I am afraid that I ignored the signs of my cancer at first, too."

Lucy was stunned. "What?"

"When I finally went to the doctor about that lump, she said it had been most likely growing for at least six months. Maybe longer. And now that I think about it, I do believe that I did notice a lump . . . but I ignored it." Looking guilty, she added, "See, I thought if I ignored it, it would go away."

Mattie's revelation forced Lucy to be completely honest, too. "The first time Paul grabbed me when I argued with him, I was shocked. Even indignant. But then, after he apologized, I convinced myself that some of the fault was mine, too. I guess I, too, tried to ignore the obvious," she added softly.

Mattie turned off the water. "So you watched and waited."

"And prayed." Lucy closed her eyes. "Mattie, you have to believe me—I didn't wish Paul harm. I didn't want him to die. I just wanted to be free. I . . . I just didn't want to hurt anymore."

"I know that," she said with an understanding smile. "But, Lucy, now you are sitting and watching everyone else move forward. Other people make plans, but you do not."

"I don't know what to hope for." Maybe she had already gotten what she'd wanted. She'd wanted to be free and happy, and now she was. To ask for more seemed like a selfish thing.

Looking somewhat like a schoolteacher, Mattie stared at her. "All you need is the freedom that will come from knowing that none of what happened was your fault. Not Paul's abuse. Not his death."

"You've told me this before, you know."

"And I'll continue to tell you until you believe me." She handed Lucy a dishrag. "This Calvin Weaver, he is a fine man. But he's only human, yes? Calvin has qualities for which to be proud of. And some other not-so-good traits, too."

"What should I do about the journal?"

"I don't know. Wait, I suppose."

"Wait for what? For Calvin to finally give me back my journal?"

With a sad smile, Mattie nodded. "That. And for him to apologize. I've known him all my life, Lucy. I promise, he's not mean-spirited. I would never let him near you if he was."

Lucy realized that was true. Mattie would protect and care for her no matter what. "So I'll wait. For a while. "

"Wait. And then maybe listen. And if it's not too hard . . . you could give him a chance."

"We have no future," Lucy said. Though she could *almost* imagine forgiving him. Almost imagine liking him. Maybe even falling in love with him. "We live far away from each other."

"People move."

"You make things sound so easy."

"Oh, life is indeed hard, but not *everything* in life is hard. If you push everything away . . . Lucy, do you feel anything for him?"

The moment she opened her mouth to say no, she felt the word stick. What she felt for Calvin was confusing, but special, too. No other man had caught her eye like he did. No other man had made her pulse race when he smiled at her.

No other man had given her so much joy in such a short amount of time.

"I do feel for him."

Mattie nodded encouragingly. "And?"

"And he's made me feel happier than I can ever remember being. He made me feel like I was important. And safe," she admitted slowly. "I almost trusted him." Swallowing, she said, "He's nothing like Paul, is he?"

"I promise you, he's not. Calvin might make mistakes, but he's a good man, Lucy." Looking beyond Lucy, Mattie lowered her voice. "You know, all this with the cancer? It's made me appreciate people more. If someone makes you happy when you're with him, and every once in a while, makes you feel *very* happy . . . then that is something to hold on to, I think."

"I think you might be right."

"Lucy, did Paul ever make you feel really happy? Even when you were courting? "

Lucy tried to remember. "Paul promised that my future would be taken care of. That's why I married him. I needed that promise." Of course, she'd later realized that his vision of the future and protection was far different from hers.

After another long look, Mattie nodded. "All right, then. I will stop hounding you. But I do think you're stronger now. Strong enough to take some chances."

"I'll do my best." Lucy kept her smile on her face as she looked over at her cousin. "Now, are you strong enough to go for a walk?"

"I am. Just a little one, though, all right?"

"That's enough for me."

Chapter 20

The pail of berries continued to be a great source of amusement at his house.

"So, Calvin?" his mother asked with a slight hint of amusement as she scrubbed the kitchen counter. "Is this pail of berries here your way of askin' me to bake you a pie?"

"Mamm, you know these berries belong to the Lapps. I'm off to go deliver it."

"Any reason you brought the pail home in the first place?"

"I was speaking with Lucy yesterday near the blackberry patch. Unfortunately, she forgot the pail when she left."

"That's a shame."

Calvin swallowed hard. His mother was trying hard not

to smile. And she obviously knew much more than she was letting on. Feeling vaguely childish, he added, "We, ah, had a small misunderstanding."

"But things are cleared up now?"

"Not yet."

As she rinsed out the sponge in the soapy water, she looked at him over her shoulder. "Care to tell me what the problem was?"

"*Nee*. It's Lucy's story to tell, not mine."

She waited a beat, looked him over. "Does her story include the fact that she was married before?"

"Yes."

"Well, Lucy's been through a difficult time, for sure. Everyone in her family was terribly worried about her, I'll tell you that."

"She is awfully young to be widowed."

His mother's brow furrowed as she scrubbed at a hardened spot on the counter. "She was awfully young for many things." After a pause, she added, "A woman like that would need a lot of patience, son."

He knew what his mother meant. It wasn't going to be enough to simply want a future with Lucy. He needed to be ready to take on her past, too.

That called for someone who was strong—and he hoped *he* would be strong enough, because Lucy needed a man who she could count on.

She'd been deeply hurt by the one person who'd promised to love and protect her, no matter what.

Quite honestly, the idea of Lucy being abused by her

husband made his blood boil. He didn't like to think of any woman trapped in a difficult marriage—but imagining Lucy in such an arrangement was especially hard.

Calvin picked up the pail. "I think I'll go deliver the berries now."

"Have a care, Calvin," she murmured. "And don't forget to keep the Lord with you. Let Him guide you in this instance."

"I always do," he replied as he carried the pail out the back door.

Only when he was walking on the path near the bushes did Calvin wonder if his mother had been talking about caring for Lucy . . . or caring for himself.

The knock at the door startled Lucy. All morning, she'd been cooking and cleaning for Mattie and her parents. Actually, her mind had been in such disarray, she'd been grateful for the work. For too many nights, she'd been dreaming about Paul.

And thinking about Calvin when the sun rose.

The knock came again.

Hurrying, she swung open the door. "Yes?"

And then she stifled a gasp as she slowly realized that the woman on the other side of the entryway was Calvin's old sweetheart.

"*Guder mariye,*" she said with a smile, just like she stopped by all the time. "You're Lucy, yes?" When she nodded, Gwen finished her introduction. "I'm Gwen Kent. I saw you when you were out shopping with your aunt, but didn't have the opportunity to introduce myself."

Lucy's eyes widened as she remembered. Mrs. Weaver had said Gwen had broken Calvin's heart.

Oh, but this was awkward! "I'm sorry, but Mattie isn't here right now."

"That's all right. Actually, I came to see you. I brought some fresh cherry bread. I hope you all will enjoy it."

"I'm sure we shall . . ." Lucy worked her bottom lip, trying to think of something to say. "Jenna took Mattie to get blood drawn. I decided to stay here and clean."

"Would you mind if I still came inside? I won't stay long. But it would be nice if we could get to know each other."

Lucy looked behind her with misgiving. "I'm afraid the house isn't in shape for guests. I was just washing the floors."

"I can help, if you'd like."

"Oh, goodness, of course you couldn't."

"Well, perhaps I could simply leave this in the kitchen for you?"

"All right. *Danke.*"

When they were in the kitchen, Gwen did her best not to step in the wet spots on the floor. After setting down her bread, she leaned back against the counter and crossed her arms.

"So what do you think of our little town of Jacob's Crossing?"

"I like it very much." Then, realizing she sounded like a ninny, she amended her words. "I mean, what I've seen of it."

"It's small, but there are many things to recommend it, I think. The downtown is pretty, with the old Methodist church buildings and the old clock tower."

"I do like that clock tower. I can't wait to hear it chime."

"You'll have to take a tour and look around some more. When you have time."

"Perhaps. But I'm here to tend to Mattie, you know."

"I'm sure she's grateful for your assistance."

"Sometimes she is . . . and sometimes I'm afraid I drive her a bit crazy."

Gwen smiled, though it didn't quite meet her eyes. Actually, she looked troubled.

"Gwen? I'm getting the feeling that you came here to speak to me about something. Is it Calvin?"

"Yes."

"We are just friends," Lucy said. "That is all."

"Actually, Calvin and I are just friends now, too." Gwen could feel her cheeks heat, so she amended her words. "I mean, I hope we will become friends again. One day."

"You are seeing someone else now, aren't you?"

"Did Calvin tell you that?"

"Mattie did."

Gwen tried to read Lucy's expression, but it was perfectly blank. "I need to marry," she said finally. "And Will, well, Will is a good man."

"Are you going to marry him?"

She nodded. "Marrying him will help my mother and sister."

As she heard those words, Lucy's world spun.

"What is wrong?" Immediately, Gwen moved closer. "Listen, I'm sorry. I meant to try to clear the air . . . but once again, I should have just let things alone."

Lucy shook her head. "No, no, that's all right. Your words just upset me, that's all."

"I'm sorry. I had heard that you and Calvin were getting closer. I don't know why I wanted to clear the air, but I think it was a silly thing to even imagine it could happen. I think I better get going." With care, she crossed the damp floor and headed to the front door. "Perhaps one day I'll stop by again. You know, to see Mattie."

"I'll let her know that."

Gwen opened the door, then stepped back. "Calvin?"

Peeking around the door, Lucy saw Calvin approach, a pail of berries in one hand and her diary in the other.

As if the situation couldn't get any more awkward. "Lucy, I brought you your berries," he called out as he approached the porch, then caught sight of her and stopped in his tracks. "Gwen? What are you doing here?"

"I was just leaving some bread for Mattie. I see you brought her some fruit."

"Actually, this was Lucy's . . ." He turned to her. "Lucy, you forgot this the other day."

"*Danke.* I can't believe I was so foolish."

"Not so much," he murmured.

Gwen looked from Calvin to Lucy and then started out the door. "Well, I think I'll be on my way. Actually, I think it's past time for me to go."

Lucy stood at the doorway as Gwen drove her buggy down the driveway. Though she hadn't been eager to speak with Gwen, she was far less eager to be alone with Calvin. The silence between them lengthened.

"I'm sorry I didn't come over last night. I should have."

Thinking of how upset she'd been, Lucy shook her head. "It was probably best you didn't."

He swallowed, gazing at her face; his expression so sweet it felt like a caress. "Yes. I—I mean, we . . ." He cleared his throat. "I mean, we probably both needed some time." Awkwardly, he handed her the diary. "I thought I'd best give this to you as well."

With shaking hands, she accepted the leather-bound book—though she was almost too embarrassed to even look at it. Hastily, she put it on the railing of the Lapps' porch.

Remembering just how she'd left him, she shrugged. "I suppose I should apologize for running off the way I did."

"Don't apologize. Everything between us, it's all my fault."

Setting the pail down, he sat on the step beside it and looked her way. "Would you mind sitting with me for a moment?"

Lucy bit her lip. She wasn't sure if she minded or not. She was still upset with him, but the all-encompassing anger and resentment she'd once felt had faded.

"Please?" he asked, his voice scratchy and soft, like the word and the emotion had been pulled from somewhere deep inside of him.

It struck a nerve, or perhaps it struck all the hopes that she'd buried deep inside of her. The hopes that one day she could sit with a man and not be afraid. Slowly, Lucy sat down next to him, primly clasping her palms over her knees. Looked straight ahead so she wouldn't be tempted to notice his blue eyes.

His muscles relaxed, making her realize that he was just as tense.

Finally, he spoke. "Lucy? Are you afraid of me?"

Startled, she turned to him. "I'm not."

"I would feel terrible if you were." Quietly, he said, "I've never laid a hand on anyone in anger. Please, believe me."

Reminding herself that she was far stronger than she used to be, Lucy forced herself to say what she was feeling. "Though I can't imagine you hitting me, I have to say that when I found out you read my journal—well, that hurt a lot. "

"I know." After a pause, he said, "Perhaps one day you'll understand that my intentions weren't cruel."

Cruel. Such a terrible, harsh word. Nerves jangling inside her, she swallowed. "I don't think you can be cruel, Calvin. I know how you were with me on the trip. And Katie, too."

"Lucy . . . Paul hurt you a lot, didn't he?"

She nodded. Oh, she ached to run away, but Lucy knew it was time to face her past, to speak about it. She couldn't continue the rest of her life reliving things she pushed to the back of her mind.

And so she gathered her courage, and spoke. "Calvin, Paul was a man who liked things his way all the time. But his wishes changed. They changed so much, I never knew what he wanted, not really." She darted a glance at Calvin.

He sat motionless, listening intently to her.

Taking a deep breath, she continued: "His moods were

mercurial. Some days, it would be fine if I only swept the floor. Other times, he yelled at me when it wasn't mopped." Lowering her voice, she added, "And one time, he made me wash it with my hands at night." She closed her eyes, hating the memories. Hating the fact that she'd sat beside him on the way to church the next day— knowing that everyone imagined he was so devout and good.

"Oh, Lucy," he murmured. "I'm so sorry." Reaching out, Calvin took her hand and placed it between his. Warming her skin, warming the bitter memories.

Another moment passed. Slowly, the painful memories lifted and she became more aware of the feeling that was brewing between the two of them.

"Lucy, do you ever think you will marry again?" he asked.

Too self-conscious to meet his gaze, she looked at their joined hands. "I don't know. I used to think I'd never marry again. That I'd never trust any man. But now . . . now I'm starting to wonder differently."

"Do you fear all men will turn into . . . a person like Paul?"

"*Nee.*" Though it was so, so hard, Lucy forced herself to keep talking. "I know enough women to realize that all men don't treat their wives like I was treated. But . . . I don't know if I will ever forget how trapped I felt." In a burst of clarity, she murmured, "That's what I'm afraid of, Calvin. I'm afraid that I won't be able to live day-to-day without fear."

"Perhaps what you need is time?"

"I suppose so." It sounded so simple, but to Lucy, it was anything but.

He released her hand and stood up.

Inwardly, Lucy sighed. He probably couldn't wait to leave. And, well, there wasn't much more to be said, anyway . . .

But instead of leaving, he reached out, clasped the pail of berries, and scooted it between them. "Calvin, what in the world?"

He grinned. "Let's start things over. Right this very moment."

"Calvin?" What was he talking about?

"How about you let me sit here with you for a while, and we just enjoy the moment? How about we just sit and eat berries?"

His comment startled a laugh—which was almost as startling as the realization that she did want to sit with him for a little bit longer. "Calvin, this is silly—"

"I don't think so."

"And I've got chores . . . Aunt Jenna's going to wonder why I didn't dust like I told her I would . . ."

"She won't care. I promise." Looking in the pail, he examined the pile of berries; then, with a satisfied look, he plucked one out. "Now *this* is a perfect blackberry."

Drawn into his silliness, Lucy examined it. Indeed, it was as perfectly formed as any she'd ever seen. And the color was a beautiful shade—right in between black and purple. "God had to be pleased with that one, for sure."

Still holding it, he looked at it this way and that. "I think you're right. Lucy, I would venture a guess that this berry right here is the best in the whole pail."

There were at least a hundred berries in that pail. "The best, hmm?"

"Do you think it's as sweet as it looks?"

"I surely have no idea."

He brought it to her lips. "Taste it and see, why don'tcha?"

Before she could stop herself, Lucy opened her lips and let Calvin feed her. She was so shocked, she closed her mouth quickly. Narrowly missing his fingers.

"Easy now," he murmured. "Don't bite the hand that feeds you. So . . . how does it taste?"

Lucy bit. Instantaneously, the bittersweet juice exploded in her mouth. Worried that juice would somehow run down her chin, she swallowed quickly. "It's delicious."

His gaze turned warmer. "I'm glad of that."

The tension between them was as electric as the lightning the night they met. Lucy was aware of every bit of him. Of the way he held his shoulders back, so proud and strong. Of his height, and his strength.

How his smiles came so easily. And how he always seemed to be aware of her. As aware as she was of him.

Seeking to keep things light, she tilted her chin up. "I'm quite sure that berry was the best of the batch."

"Well, we'll just have to see about that," he replied, his eyes sparkling. After choosing another, he popped one into his own mouth. "Hmm . . . maybe I was wrong. This one was pretty good, too."

Unable to stop herself, she started laughing. "Calvin Weaver, what am I going to do with you?"

"Sit here and eat berries with me. Just for a little while." His expression earnest, he eyed her. "Can you do that,

Lucy? Can you just sit with me for a little while and enjoy the day?"

She had things to do. They had things to talk about.

But none of that seemed as important as sitting next to him, as feeling that same little rush of emotion that she'd now come to anticipate whenever he was near. "You know what? I can sit with you for a spell," she said, plucking out a berry for herself. "I would very much like to enjoy the day. At least for a little while."

Calvin nodded. "Then that's what we'll do."

Chapter 21

"Mattie, your blood counts are low today. I think we'd better watch over you for a while this evening," Dr. Wilmington, her oncologist, said when he entered her examining room.

Mattie nodded even as her world spun. Perhaps she shouldn't have been surprised? For the last few days she'd felt terrible—even worse than usual. Plus, she was tired. So, so tired.

Beside her, Lucy hopped to her feet. "Doctor, the low blood counts—what does that mean?"

"It means Mattie's body might not be responding to the chemo drugs as well as I would have hoped," he said quietly. "I want to run a few more tests and monitor some things. We can't do that in an office visit."

"Oh," Lucy said.

Feeling her cousin's gaze settle on her, Mattie knew she should say something. Try to reassure her. But unfortunately, she just couldn't do it.

Instead, she bit her lip as Lucy's jaw tightened and her voice turned cheerful and optimistic. "Well, this is for the best, then, ain't so, Mattie?"

Was it? Mattie only shrugged and looked out the window as Dr. Wilmington was already murmuring orders to the nurse who had just entered.

When the nurse exited the room, Lucy stepped forward and started pestering the doctor again. "Dr. Wilmington, has Mattie gotten worse?" she asked, just as if Mattie wasn't sitting there right next to her. "Is something terribly wrong?"

"Not necessarily." While Dr. Wilmington went into a long and drawn-out explanation about numbers and platelets to Lucy—who must had been studying up on such things because she kept interrupting and asking for clarification—Mattie let her mind wander.

Instead of concentrating on the state of her blood, she thought about her garden. Wondered when her daisies and black-eyed Susans would bloom. Thought about getting a hydrangea bush. She did so love its violet blooms.

As Lucy and the doctor continued to weigh the pros and cons of her treatment, Mattie daydreamed about gardening. Oh, she hoped that one day soon she could kneel in the soft dirt and feel the sun on her back again. That she could dig her hands into the earth and not have to worry about getting an infection.

Dreaming about nature was the best way to get through

the day. She'd already learned that even the best of explanations could never tell her exactly what she wanted to know—and that was why in the world a twenty-two-year-old woman would be struck with cancer.

When his speech wound down, and Lucy looked more confused than ever, a silence permeated the room.

Obviously, both Lucy and the doctor were waiting for her to say something. Anything to illustrate her understanding. With a sigh, Mattie faced the inevitable. "I'm going to be here longer than just one night, aren't I?"

The kind doctor's eyes softened. Like he understood just what a hardship it was for her. "I think so." Looking down at her chart, he murmured, "Your body is having a difficult reaction to some of the drugs. I'm worried about your swollen hands and feet."

Looking at her hands, which were indeed terribly red and swollen, Mattie nodded. She'd been worried about them, too . . . but hadn't wanted to say anything.

"We'll cross our fingers that your stay will be just for one night," Dr. Wilmington said. "I'm hoping the change in the dosage of your medicine will alleviate the problems. But we'll need to keep a close eye on you. We can't be too careful, you know."

"I suppose not." Looking Lucy's way, she added drily, "I'll cross my fingers, too."

"And you will pray, too, yes?" Lucy asked in Pennsylvania Dutch.

"Of course," she replied. But of course that was a lie. She wouldn't be praying. Praying didn't help.

"Mattie, after you're admitted and we get more of your

tests results back, I'll stop by your room," Dr. Wilmington said. "In the meantime, do you have any more questions?"

"*Nee.*" After all, there was really nothing to say.

Gently patting her arm, he smiled at both her and Lucy, then exited.

In a furtive motion, Lucy wiped her eyes. Mattie pretended she didn't see, though her heart went out to her cousin. It was difficult to hear such bad news. Especially the first time. So she attempted to lighten things up. "Well, there goes our fun afternoon."

But instead of Lucy joking right back, she flinched. "Mattie, I'm worried about you."

"Don't you worry none. There're lots and lots of people who are watching every little part of me, Lucy. I'll be okay."

"It's not your cancer I'm worried about, it's your feelings."

"My feelings?" Mattie raised an eyebrow. "My feelings don't matter, Lucy."

"Of course they do. Why, it's your spirit and your hope that are the most important right now." Looking her over, Lucy's eyes narrowed. "You're not giving up, are you?"

"Of course not."

"You better not. Things will get better, I promise. They always do."

Mattie wished her mind was clearer. Her cousin had a tender heart, and only wanted to make things better. The right thing to do would be to offer some kind of consolation. Something to ease Lucy's worries and make sure her cousin would believe that everything was going to be all rosy. But at the moment, Mattie didn't have anything more to say. The disease was taking over her life, bit by bit.

She used to feel she was so strong. She used to feel like she could do anything—even fix Lucy's life. Even fix Lucy.

Now it was all too apparent that she couldn't even fix herself.

Looking at her light teal dress lying on the back of Lucy's chair, she mused, "Do you think I could get dressed? I hate these thin hospital gowns they make me wear."

Lucy brightened. "Yes, changing would be better. I'll go ask."

But just as she opened the door, another nurse popped through.

"Mattie, I heard you're going to visit with us for a few days," she said, her voice crisp.

"I heard that as well." Desperately, she looked at her dress. If she had on her clothes, at least she could still be herself on the outside. "Can I get dressed?"

"There's no need, dear. We're going to call in an orderly to help move you to a wheelchair. Then we'll transfer you from the medical center to the main hospital building."

With a sympathetic look, Lucy said, "My cousin will be cold dressed just in that gown . . ."

"Oh, we'll cover you up in warm blankets," the nurse replied as she moved around the room, gathering Mattie's things into a neat pile. "Don't you worry, dear. We'll have you snug as a bug, head to toe."

Mattie sighed as depression weighed down on her again. Though her brain told her everything the nurse said made sense, it was never more evident that she was supposed to do nothing but sit and follow directions.

As Lucy asked about a phone and the nurse told her the way to the nurses' station, Mattie only half listened.

Even though the doctors said it was all gone, the cancer was still winning. It didn't matter how she'd gotten it. What mattered was that she did.

All she had to understand was that it had claimed her, and it wanted to be the winner. She was the loser.

She could put up a brave front. She could act like she was fighting her hard battle—and she would. But now Mattie knew for certain—felt it deep inside her—that the cancer was going to claim her life.

Prayer worked wonders, John thought as he sat in the empty sanctuary of the Lutheran church and breathed deep. Ever since Calvin and Katie had stopped by to tell him about Mattie's turn for the worse, it had weighed heavily on his mind.

A part of him knew it didn't make all that much sense. Though he'd met Mattie when he walked over to the Lapps' with Graham, he truly didn't know the girl all that well.

He didn't know her any better than the dozens of people he'd met over the last few years. Some of them had been really hurting, too. But he'd never been tempted to pray for them.

However, he felt closer to everyone here in Jacob's Crossing. Even though he wasn't living at his old house, he felt a part of the community. And because of that, he ached to do anything to help their worries.

Even if it was only prayers.

Obediently, he prayed for Mattie's health. And for her doctors and nurses and other caregivers. He prayed for Mattie's parents, and for everyone who was working so hard to make each of her days a little easier.

He gave thanks for God's healing touch. And for all the blessings in his life.

And then he paused.

As the moments passed, John was sure he felt the Lord Himself standing at his side, waiting for the rest of the truth.

"Lord, I guess I can't fool you, can I?" he murmured. "You're right. I'm here for selfish reasons, too. I need help and guidance."

As the air around him softened, John kept talking. "Lord, I know coming back to Jacob's Crossing was the right thing to do. I am so thankful to be forging a relationship with my brother's family. They are good people, and a true joy to me."

"And this donut shop, well, it's a gift. I am enjoying my partnership with Amos, and I am certainly happy to not be working in a cubicle like I was in Indy."

"So I'm real thankful for all of that."

He took a deep breath. "But, God, I just don't understand why you've brought two such different women into my life. What can it mean? Jayne is everything I used to dream about. An English woman, confident, beautiful. Okay, I'll admit it—she's desirable. Very much so."

Feeling a bit embarrassed to admit such things aloud, he rushed on. "But, Lord, Mary has taken my heart, too. Every time I see her, I want to do more for her. I want to help her with Abel, and hear more about her life . . . And how can that be? I left the order.

"I left, and I didn't look back. Well, not until now.

"What do you want me to do?"

John paused, half waiting for a bolt of lightning or a note to fly through the air, giving him specific directions.

But of course nothing like that came. No, all he felt was a reassurance that he wasn't alone. That his prayers would be heard.

In due time.

"Amen," John said. Standing up, he looked around and realized he felt a little bit better. No, nothing was decided, and he was still as confused as ever.

But at least he felt like he had a buddy to discuss things with.

Chapter 22

After much deliberation, Mattie came to the conclusion that God must have, indeed, decided to leave her. She'd tried to pray, but that had been hopeless. For the first time in her life, she'd felt only emptiness when she'd prayed. As if no one was listening, that no one really cared.

Perhaps that was for the best?

Accepting the harsh reality of her situation seemed like the only way to survive. Now that she had stopped fighting the inevitable, and had stopped feeling so sorry for herself, Mattie realized she could concentrate on the needs of other people.

Which was a welcome change.

Now that she wasn't consumed with herself, Mattie could look around and take in her surroundings. And what she saw there was amazing. She knew she was witnessing the Lord's work in almost everything at the hospital.

Yes, God was working with the doctors and nurses. He was guiding them, giving them the knowledge to treat the cancer cells in their patients' bodies. He gave the volunteers the strength to continually smile even when many of the patients were difficult and short-tempered.

He guided the technicians who worked in the radiation labs. The Lord was surely with Charlie, their driver, too. Miraculously, he never lost his patience, even when both she and her mother were not at their best.

All this thinking about others did give her comfort, and it did hold threads of hope for her, too. God was there in the hospital with them.

And just because He wasn't watching over her, it didn't mean He didn't care about others.

That knowledge made her stay almost bearable.

That, and her loving cousin Lucy.

Oh, but she couldn't help but worry about Lucy. Over the last three days, Lucy had left only once. Otherwise, she bustled and fetched. Smiled and encouraged. But not this afternoon.

"What is bothering you so much, Lucy?"

Lucy blinked. "Nothing."

"Please tell me."

"It's just that I never imagined your healing would be such a roller coaster event. That's all. I had thought that we would get through your chemotherapy treatments and then you would be better."

Mattie completely understood. "All this, it was hard for

me to accept at first, too. But I've come to find out that this cancer is a mighty tough opponent. Wily, too."

"I don't know how to make things better for you."

"You already have made things better by being here." Mattie was being completely honest. Lucy's presence had been a true gift.

Slowly, Lucy nodded. "I'm glad I am here." Standing up, she shook out her skirts. "Now, how can I help you?"

Though Mattie didn't really feel like being fussed over, she saw that Lucy ached to do something—anything—to feel useful. So she pointed to her head and frowned. "My hair's an awful mess. Would you mind brushing it out for me?"

"Not at all." After digging through Mattie's suitcase, Lucy helped Mattie off with her *kapp*, then unpinned her hair.

When her hair fell in waves down her shoulders, Mattie smiled. Perhaps a good hair brushing was what she needed. She closed her eyes when Lucy started.

As the soft bristles rubbed against her head, she felt her shoulder and neck muscles relax. It had been a long time since anyone had brushed her hair. Years.

Ah. Yes, this was most likely what she needed—to take time to enjoy the simple pleasure of getting her hair brushed.

And then she could put her *kapp* back on, and she would look more like herself. Neat and orderly.

"Oh, my," Lucy murmured. Quietly. So quietly, Mattie almost didn't hear her.

"What?"

With a stricken look, Lucy held up a handful of hair. "It's coming out."

Mattie grabbed the brush. "What is? My hair?" she asked, but of course it was a silly thing to ask. She knew what was happening.

"I'm sorry, Mattie. I'm afraid the medicine is causing it to come out."

Awkwardly, Mattie ran the brush along her scalp. To her dismay, thick strands of hair came out. Right into her hands. Some fell onto her lap.

Crushed, she examined the rich brown strands now lying limp in her hands. Though she had never been an especially prideful girl, she'd always rather liked her hair. She'd liked the rich chocolate color and how thick and long it was.

And now it was falling out. Showing her once and for all that the cancer was winning another battle. And proving that God was still looking the other way.

"Lucy, go find me a mirror, would ya?"

"Oh, no . . ."

"Please?" Mattie couldn't help that her voice had gotten high and shrill. "Please? Now. I can't get up easily with the cords attached to me."

"All right," Lucy said. With another look of dismay, she met Mattie's eyes, then swallowed hard. Without another word, she practically ran out the door.

Unable to help herself, Mattie brushed at her head again. Harder this time. In retaliation, more strands pulled away.

Minutes later, Lucy came in with a handheld mirror, and a concerned-looking nurse on her heels.

"Mattie, why don't you put that brush away? We don't need to dwell—"

She held out her hand. "Please. Give me the mirror."

But instead of handing the mirror forward, Lucy looked at the nurse.

"It's all right," the nurse said quietly. "Let Mattie have it."

With obvious reluctance, Lucy did as she bid.

Half dreading what she would see, Mattie raised it to her face. Immediately she spied a gray patch of bare skin that was now showing just above her ear. Unable to stop her sounds of dismay, Mattie tilted her head and moved the mirror around. More patches were visible.

And even more strands were loose in her hair, just waiting to fall on her lap. The tears now fell on her cheeks. She was in a losing battle with the disease. First it had claimed her breast, and now her hair. Already she'd lost ten pounds.

She was turning into someone she didn't know. "I'm *hatt gukkich*."

"You are not," Lucy said. "You are not ugly at all."

"Why don't you let me have the mirror now, child," the nurse said gently.

Though she wanted to scream and fight, Mattie did as she was bid.

When the nurse held the mirror again, she gazed at her with concern. "I can give you some medicine for your anxiety. It will help you rest."

"I don't need medicine. I'm fine."

"All right," she said agreeably. "Now, would you care to pin your hair back up and put it under your *kapp*?"

Mattie struggled with a reply. At the moment, she was afraid to touch her head. Afraid doing so would only pull out more strands.

After a meaningful look Lucy's way, the nurse said, "Or we could do something else . . ."

"And what is that?"

"We could go get Miss Beverly. She's a volunteer hair-dresser."

The nurse made no sense. "Why in the world would I need—"

"Miss Beverly shaves heads for women who are losing their hair," she explained. "She's here today. I saw her just down the hall."

Oh, but shaving her head seemed like a terribly hard step.

But even if she fought the changes, they would still come. The chemo would still take its toll. "If you could find this Miss Beverly, I would be most appreciative," she said quietly.

"I'll be right back, sugar," the nurse said with a smile.

Lucy walked around the bed and sat at her side. "Oh, Mattie, I'm so, so sorry."

Mattie was, too. She was sorry about her hair, and her looks. And the fact that once again, her faith felt so tenuous.

Just when she was about to remind Lucy that God was in charge . . . Mattie was coming to realize that she didn't care for that arrangement. Not at all.

Not one little bit.

* * *

Focus on Mattie. She needs you. Focus on her needs, not yours.

Over and over again, Lucy repeated the mantra, willing herself to believe the words. Willing herself to let them guide her.

Focusing on Mattie helped keep her mind off Calvin. All their misconceptions about each other had fallen away on the steps, leaving room for their feelings to grow.

And now they seemed to be in full bloom. No, it was more than that. She'd felt happy and calm. And peaceful. And for one little moment . . . the only thing she'd thought about was Calvin. And the fact that she was sure he'd been about to kiss her.

And if he had, Lucy knew she would have kissed him back. The feelings had been mildly shocking. When Paul died, she had sworn to herself that she'd never trust a man again. Certainly, she'd promised herself to never get involved in another relationship! All that would bring her was sorrow and pain.

So why did she now find herself thinking about him all the time?

"Lucy?" Mattie asked, snapping back her attention.

"Yes?"

"I . . . I don't want to get my head shaved." A new shadow of pain lit her eyes. "I'm afraid."

"Of course you are," Lucy murmured as she sat on her bed and, with her hands, gently embraced Mattie's face. "It's a scary thing, this is."

"What if it doesn't grow back?"

Afraid to assure her about something she knew nothing

of, Lucy murmured, "Have you ever heard of someone's hair not returning?"

"*Nee.*" Mattie seemed to shrink into herself. "I'm just sad and angry that all this is happening to me. I know it's selfish."

"You're not selfish, Mattie," Lucy consoled. "You're just trying to come to grips with a mighty hard day. That's all."

Mattie squeezed her hand. "How bad does my head look . . . really?"

"It looks bad, Mattie. Not *gut* at all."

"You never did pussyfoot around the truth, did you?"

"Oh, I have. There were times with Paul that I got terribly *gut* at hiding bad things." Remembering another visit, Lucy said, "Do you recall when you came to see me right after you heard about Paul's death?"

"Of course."

"And do you remember when you knocked on my door to see if I needed help?"

After a moment, realization dawned. "And I discovered the bruises and faded marks on your skin?"

Lucy nodded.

"I remember."

"I remember you telling me that perhaps I shouldn't waste too many more tears on a man who had made me look so bad."

Mattie's lips curved up. "And, oh, but you did look bad, Lucy. And I told you so."

"Sometimes honesty is what we need to hear, Cousin."

"So you think I should let this Miss Beverly cut off my hair?"

"I do. It will make things easier, I think. And perhaps it will be something else you can cross off your list to dread."

As if on cue, Mattie's door opened and an attractive *Englischer* lady carrying a bright pink tote bag appeared in the doorway. "Knock, knock," she said with a smile. "May I come in?"

Lucy looked to Mattie.

After a moment's pause, she nodded. "Please."

"My name is Beverly." She paused at the foot of Mattie's bed. "I'm a volunteer here. For years, I owned my own hair salon. Now I help patients in any way I can." With a compassionate look, she murmured, "The nurse said you might have need of my services. Do you?"

With a feeling of fate, Mattie nodded, keeping her eyes straight ahead. She knew that if she looked Lucy's way, she would dissolve into tears. Steadying her voice, and speaking as calmly and stoically as she possibly could, she said, "This is a wonderful-*gut* service you offer."

The hairdresser's cheek dimpled. "My sister is a cancer survivor. Years ago, after she recovered, I mentioned to her that I wished I could have done more to help others in some way. She suggested this. I'm trying to make a difficult situation just a bit easier."

Mattie focused on the lady's words as she pulled out her scissors; and Lucy held her hand as the first snip was made next to her ear. Then Mattie gave in to temptation and let her eyes close when the electric clipper was plugged in and Miss Beverly began to shave off the remains of her hair.

"Focus on the future," Lucy murmured. "Focus on the future, not what is happening now."

Mattie didn't need to be told that Lucy was drawing on her own personal experiences for that advice.

However, at the moment, she couldn't see a future. Instead, it was just a looming, dark cloud. Dark and foreboding and thick. And not allowing even a patch of sunlight to peek through.

Chapter 23

Calvin and Graham were sitting on Mattie's front porch when the van dropped them off.

"What are they doing here?" Mattie asked Lucy, her voice cracking. "Why did they come?"

"I'm sure they just want to see how you are doing."

"Obviously not well," Mattie said bitterly.

Through the open door, Lucy glanced at the men. They were looking at Mattie, specifically her bald head. Before he could hide it, a flash of pain entered Graham's eyes.

After Lucy paid Charlie and helped Mattie out, she leaned close to her cousin. "Would you like me to ask them to leave? I can . . . if that's what you want."

But before Mattie could reply, both men were at their side. Graham placed one arm around Mattie's waist, offering support. Calvin was reaching into the back and picking up their suitcases. "Don't make us leave," Graham said to Lucy. "We saw your aunt at the market earlier today. She's the one who told us you two were due back around two this afternoon."

Mattie hung her head.

When both men looked at her in alarm, Lucy attempted to smile. "Here, it is almost four! Have you been waiting this whole time?"

Calvin nodded. "Pretty much."

"That was mighty kind of you," Lucy murmured, looking hesitantly Mattie's way.

Mattie still stayed silent, her head toward the ground. Her *kapp* looked strange and loose on her bald head.

Wordlessly, Lucy looked at the men, aching for them to say something comforting but having no idea what they could possibly say to make things better.

Then, to Lucy's amazement, Graham placed one finger under Mattie's chin and raised it until he was looking directly into her eyes. "Mattie, you know I wouldn't be able to stay away. I wanted to see your new look."

Calvin stiffened. "Graham," he chided.

Lucy was just about to pull her cousin away, to quickly shuttle her inside—and away from Graham's hurtful tongue—when the most surprising thing happened. Mattie stood up straighter.

"I canna believe you said that, Graham Weaver," she said, her eyes flashing.

Not looking the least bit apologetic, he shrugged. "I had to say something."

"It couldn't have been something nice?"

Again, Graham surprised them all by chuckling. "*Nee.* I wanted to see the spark in your eyes." He winked. "And there it is once again," he said, sounding genuinely pleased. "Now you are finally looking at me with your pretty brown eyes. I thought you were gonna ignore me until we got into your house." Looking at both Lucy and Calvin, he motioned for them to walk behind as he and Mattie entered the house.

Though Lucy ached to protect her, she did as Graham bid. He was able to do something that she had not been able to do the whole journey home—get Mattie to speak.

Lucy and Calvin kept some distance as Mattie and Graham continued speaking.

"I have no hair," her cousin whined as they went into the entryway.

"I know," he said gently.

"I look awful."

"You look mighty different, but maybe not 'awful.' Actually, you just look like Mattie with no hair."

Lucy shared a smile with Calvin as Mattie protested. "Graham—"

"Shh, now. All it means to me is that the medicine is helping your cancer stay away. Now, let me help you to the couch."

"Will you stay for a while?"

"I will."

Soon, they moved too far into the house for Lucy and Calvin to hear another word.

Now that she knew her cousin was in good hands, Lucy

sighed with relief. It had been a long few days. "I have to say it, Calvin. Your brother Graham is a gift from heaven right now."

Calvin chuckled. "You might be the first person besides my *mamm* to ever call him that."

"I tried the whole way home to get her to talk about how she was feeling, but she refused," she said as she joined him on the stoop.

"We got lucky. When Jenna told us about your phone call, and about Mattie's hair, we knew we had to do something." Looking contemplative, Calvin corrected himself. "Well, Graham insisted that we come over and wait."

"He's such a good friend to her."

"No less than you, Lucy."

She shivered. At the moment, she felt completely ineffective. "I could hardly get her to say a word the whole way home."

"Sometimes talking isn't needed, though, you know?"

"Is that why you came, too?"

"Partly. I also wanted to check on you." As if it was the most natural thing in the world, Calvin reached for her hand and enfolded it in his. "Are you all right, Lucy?"

She couldn't seem to think about anything other than how warm his skin was. How gentle his grip was. "Me? I'm fine."

"I just wanted to be sure. It's hard work, being strong all the time, you know."

Feeling so secure, and feeling yet another shiver of awareness at his touch, Lucy finally let her guard down.

"To be honest, it's been a hard few days. All the medical tests and terms are confusing. And Mattie, of course, was *naerfich* and afraid."

"Anyone would be nervous and afraid, I think."

"Well, let me just say that it's a blessing you and your brother were here. I've been walking on eggshells around Mattie's bald head. One minute it would seem like it didn't bother her, then next it looked liked tears were going to flow at any minute. My way of dealing with it was to not mention it, I suppose. But I think Graham's teasing helped her more."

"She and Graham have been friends for a mighty long time. He always seems to know what is best for Mattie."

"It seems like more than that . . ."

Calvin shook his head. "It's not. They've never had any interest in anything other than friendship."

"Sometimes things change."

"Sometimes they do, but I don't think their relationship will change much. They value their friendship, and that's a *gut* thing."

"You're right about that." Looking hard at Calvin, she said, "Are you ever going to talk to me about what happened between Gwen and Will?"

His grip tightened, then loosened as he visibly controlled his response. "There is nothing to say."

"I've heard rumors, Calvin. Are you sure you are over her?"

For a few minutes, Calvin said nothing. Just stared out at the fields in front of them, lost in thought. Then he looked her way. "Gwen and I were courting for some time. Then one day, she handed me a note."

"What did it say?"

"It said that she didn't want me anymore, if you want to know the truth. It said that she and Will were happier with each other than she had been with me."

"What did you do?"

"Me? Nothing."

"You didn't confront the two of them?"

"No. There was no need. What's done was done."

Her heart went out to him. She knew what it was like to count on something, just to have it all go sour. But, as she thought of how hard she'd tried with Paul, Lucy couldn't help but feel that Calvin had given up too easily.

"Calvin, if you still love her, you should fight for her, don't you think?"

"I don't love her. Now that I think about it, I don't think I ever did. And as for Will . . . well, I would never fight my best friend." He got to his feet in a rush. "It's all over, Lucy. It's done. Gwen found someone else, and had found someone else for some time before she told me. She lied to me. So did Will. And when I discovered the truth, there was nothing left to do but to live with their decisions."

He exhaled and started pacing. "Gwen and Will's friendship are part of my past, not my future. And there's no point complaining and wishing things were different. All I have to do is find a way to live with it." He stepped away, his body matching the emotional distance that had formed between the two of them.

Still sitting, Lucy looked at his broad shoulders and straight back and thought about how strong he was. He was a man who could handle many burdens. But there was more to him than strength. He could be hurt, too. But instead of hurting back, he swallowed the pain.

"Calvin . . . ?"

After what felt like forever, he turned to her again. Lucy saw the tension in his face and knew he was waiting for her to tease him about being jilted.

Or to chide him about not sharing more of his feelings. But she knew all about hiding feelings . . . and having them discovered. And along the way, she'd also come to understand that keeping bad things hidden didn't make them any easier to deal with.

It just made them harder to face.

Quietly, she stood up and crossed the short distance to him. "Though you came over here for Mattie's sake . . . I'm glad you did. It was *gut* to see you today." And because she was eager to touch him, to reassure, she pressed her hands to his upper arms. Just for a second. Just enough to show him that she cared.

Bit by bit, the wariness that had frozen his expression thawed and that longing she'd spied earlier reappeared. "I'm glad you are glad, Lucy." Reaching out, he trailed his fingers down her arm. "I'm probably doing this all wrong— but I want you to know . . . I can't seem to stop thinking about you." A half smile formed on his lips as his fingers linked through hers again. "Or touching you."

Daring to smile, she shook her head. She liked his touch. And she loved that he was thinking about her. After all, she hadn't been able to stop thinking about him. "You aren't doing this all wrong at all. For the first time, everything feels right."

With care, Calvin wrapped his arms around her and enfolded her in a hug. His arms were loose, giving her space and the choice to step away.

But Lucy didn't want to. Instead of moving away, she rested her head on his shoulder. Inhaling, she smelled his clean scent. Felt the muscles of his chest under her cheek.

And for the first time in days—or maybe it was years?—Lucy felt at peace.

Chapter 24

Calvin noticed his gloves were caked with mud when they were already halfway to Wal-Mart. As he kept a firm hand on Beauty, while waiting at a stoplight, he couldn't help but stare at the worn leather: The gloves were stiff and uncomfortable; tiny bits of dirt flew off of them each time he clutched the reins. Truly, he should have cleaned them before the drive. Why was he just now noticing their state?

"*Calvin.* The light has turned," his mother gently prodded.

After making sure no cars had run the light, he motioned Beauty forward.

"You seem more quiet than usual today. Is something wrong?"

"Nothing of importance."

"How is the plowing coming along?"

"About the same as ever. Slow."

"Perhaps the rain will come soon. We could use it."

"It would be a blessing," he mumbled, suddenly recalling how much he'd hoped for an end to the storms when he'd traveled east on the train.

"Calvin, I was hoping that after we shop we could have lunch together."

He had hoped to get back home and help Loyal clean the plow. Loyal had taken over the plowing when he'd left, but Calvin knew it would take both of them at least two hours to wash it up and the other farm implements.

"If you'd like to have lunch, then we shall. Where would you like to go?"

"To Applebee's."

"No Amish cooking for you, hmm?"

"I have had more than enough Amish food in my house, Calvin. I'm looking forward to their pasta."

"Well, I could have some of that. Or Mexican food, maybe?"

As he'd expected, his mother's eyes lit up. "Oh, yes. I read about green enchiladas in a magazine the other day. Doesn't that sound interesting?"

Personally, the only green food Calvin trusted was a vegetable. "Enchiladas do sound interesting . . ."

"Did John take you to lots of restaurants in Indianapolis?"

"He did. Katie's favorite was an ice cream parlor. They had thirty-one flavors there."

The expression of wonder on her mother's face was almost comical. "Oh, Calvin. What were some of the flavors?"

Her comments were enough to make him smile for the last twenty minutes of the trip.

When they reached Wal-Mart, he helped her out of the buggy, then motioned her forward. "Mamm, I'm going to stay out here for a while. Take your time, though."

She faltered. "You sure?"

"Positive. I'm going to try to clean up my boots and gloves a bit," he said as an excuse. "If I went inside with them like this, they'd surely leave a trail of mud wherever I went."

"You might have a point about that. Calvin, going out caked in mud isn't like you. Are you all right?"

"I'm fine. Don't worry."

"All right . . . if you're sure?"

"I'm sure."

After another curious look his way, she left his side and went into the store. And then Calvin felt like he could finally exhale.

Ever since he'd left Lucy's side yesterday, their conversation—and the way they'd stood together in silence—haunted him.

Something special was happening between them, something—like the mechanical problems on the train—that was out of his control.

But unlike the train's malfunctions, this new development between him and Lucy made him feel happy—and long for something more. In their short association, they'd already been challenged. But now things were on track. He couldn't help but think about a future with Lucy in it.

A future of making her smile.

"Calvin?"

"Hmm?" He looked up, his mind still on Lucy . . . and that dimple in her cheek. Then he froze when he realized Will was standing in front of him. "Will. Hello." Against his best efforts, Calvin scanned the man who used to be his best friend.

Will stood tall and straight in front of him, his looks as chiseled as ever. But there was a new vulnerability in his eyes.

Slowly, Calvin walked forward. Though he still resented the way Will and Gwen had begun their relationship, he knew they would be crossing paths often. They had to be as civil as possible. "What brings you here?"

Will shrugged. "The same thing that brings everyone else here, I imagine. Paper towels and toilet paper."

Calvin couldn't help but grin. More of the anger and resentment slowly dissipated, uncovering the bare bones of their friendship.

Maybe it was intact after all.

"I brought my mother here to shop. You know how much she likes coming here."

Will grinned. "Everyone knows how much your mother likes this supercenter." After a pause, Will added, "I heard you went to Indianapolis."

"I did."

"And got stuck on the train on the way home?"

"You heard correctly," Calvin replied, then waited. He knew Will's tic in his cheek well. He had something on his mind and he was figuring out a way to say it.

"So . . . you ever plannin' to forgive me for keeping company with Gwen?"

"Forgive you for keeping company with her behind my back, you mean?"

"It wasn't like that."

"What was it like?"

That muscle in Will's cheek jumped again. "Gwen and me, we didn't plan on falling in love. We just did." Meeting his gaze, Will shrugged. "I didn't intend for it to happen. I hope one day you'll believe me."

Calvin's pride wanted him to argue and complain. But if he was honest with himself, he knew Will was right. Sometimes love did happen, right when a person least expected it. Just like things had happened with him and Lucy.

As the silence, and the tension, between them grew, Calvin knew it was time to forgive. Making the decision, he held out his hand. "I wish the best for you both."

Stepping forward, Will shook his hand. *"Danke."*

"So . . . I should go find my mother. You know, there's no telling what she'll put in her cart."

Will's eyes sparkled. "Probably a *gut* idea." He rocked back on his heels. "See you at church?"

"Of course."

After a nod, Will turned around and disappeared through the doors of the store. Leaving Calvin feeling like a load had been lifted from his shoulders. He now almost believed that time really did heal all wounds.

Chapter 25

All day women had bustled around the Lapps' kitchen, making casseroles for the coming week, but now, it seemed, most had left. Of course, they'd also left a bit of a mess.

Mentally, Lucy figured she had just under an hour to get the kitchen to rights before Mattie and Aunt Jenna returned. But when she went back to her aunt's kitchen, Lucy skittered to a stop.

Gwen was still there.

It was tempting to turn back around, but of course, that wasn't the right thing to do. She had come to Mattie's home to help, and that's what she had done.

With that in mind, Lucy stepped forward. "Thank you for staying a little longer."

"I don't mind. As I told Mattie, I want to help in any way I can."

"I don't mind at all," Lucy replied. "There's so much to do."

"And no one in the Lapp family ever asks for help."

"I've thought that same thing," Lucy said, sharing a smile with the other girl.

Well, maybe she was finally going to be able to cast away her wariness around Gwen. Breathing deep, Lucy gave thanks for Psalm 51: *Create in me a clean heart, O God. Renew a loyal spirit within me.*

Yes, it truly wasn't her place to judge what had happened between Gwen and Calvin. She needed to keep that in the forefront of her mind, above all else.

Gwen looked up from the orange she was sectioning. "So many people have brought Jenna and Mattie fresh fruit, I thought I'd make a fruit salad."

"I'll help you, if I may." After washing her hands and claiming one of Jenna's paring knives, Lucy took her place beside Gwen and started slicing strawberries. "Mattie should enjoy this," she said after a moment. "She likes fruit salad very much."

"She always took care to tell me that she got oranges at Christmas," Gwen murmured. "I hope she still likes them."

"Mattie told me some things don't taste like they used to. But we can only try, I suppose."

Gwen frowned. "Yes, that is all we can do."

Looking for a happier topic, Lucy said, "I heard that you will be getting married soon."

"Yes." She added quickly, "Have you met Will?"

"I'm sorry, I have not."

"I'll look forward to introducing you to him, then." She paused. "He's a *gut* man."

"I'm happy for you."

Gwen set her knife down. "I'm glad to hear that," she said slowly. "I thought perhaps you would be angry at me on Calvin's behalf."

Because she'd been tempted to be that way, Lucy knew her cheeks were flushing. "Your relationships are none of my concern. After all, I hardly know Calvin."

"Really? I had gotten the feeling that you knew each other quite well."

Gwen was right. Lucy did know Calvin fairly well. But they'd had their moments of confusion, too. "Gwen, if you don't mind me asking . . . why did you choose Will?"

"I chose Will because he chose me," she said after a pause. "And we fell in love. And . . . because it is necessary that I marry."

Ah. There was that mention again.

Lucy gripped the handle on her knife as she recalled her early feelings of duty and responsibility. "I married like that as well."

Beside her, Gwen froze. "I didn't know you were married."

"He died." Lucy didn't dare turn to meet her gaze, though. She was afraid if she did, she would never be able to tell her story. And instinctively she knew that the Lord had provided her with this moment with Gwen just for this purpose. "I don't like to speak of it."

"Because you miss him too much?"

Oh, but Gwen's voice had a wistful edge to it. Lucy was

almost tempted to let her think that way. It would be easier.

But it wouldn't be the truth.

"No, that isn't the reason." She cleared her throat. "I'm the oldest of six children. My family was having some financial struggles. Moving out and moving on seemed the right thing to do."

"Those feelings are understandable."

Lucy felt her insides relax, glad to be understood. "*Jah*. Paul was a handsome man, and very personable. My family enjoyed his company. It seemed like an easy choice."

Gwen paused. "So you two were happy?"

Lucy closed her eyes as she tried to recall her feelings for the man who ultimately did so much to harm her. "No. No, we were not."

Then, remembering that God was right beside her, Lucy forced herself to continue. "Gwen, I had a child's view of love and marriage. I imagined that Paul and I would somehow have a houseful of *kinner*, and that in many ways we would have separate lives. He would go to work at the ironworks, and I would stay home and raise the children."

"But that didn't happen?"

"Oh, nothing happened like I imagined. Living with someone is a difficult thing, Gwen. Even in the best of relationships, each person must compromise and give and take. But Paul wasn't like that. He liked always being right." She paused, trying to come up with the correct words, but there really weren't any. "Paul liked being in charge, and he was angry and hurtful . . . and he liked hurting me."

Gwen paled. "What did your family do?"

"Nothing."

"But—"

"I hid a lot of my problems. After all, there was nothing they could do. I was Paul's wife. I'd spoken vows and I promised I would honor and obey him." In spite of the gravity of the conversation, Lucy smiled. "This is what I'm trying to tell you, Gwen. At the end of the day, it doesn't really matter what everyone else thinks you should do, or wants you to do. If you marry the wrong person, you, and you alone, will have to deal with the consequences, in every way possible."

"Are you saying you think I shouldn't want to marry Will?"

"I'm not saying that at all. I don't know you or Will. I'm no judge." She swallowed, prayed for the Lord to help her with her words. To help her find the right words. "But, Gwen, I found out the hard way that marrying Paul in order to help my family didn't end up helping them at all. My parents knew I was unhappy and felt guilty. My siblings knew I had married in order to help them and they felt a lot of grief, too."

"What happened to Paul?"

"One evening, he slipped on a ladder and fell." Just in time, she closed her mouth. The last thing she wanted to do was to admit her guilt. To admit that she should have checked on him far earlier than she did.

"And then you were free."

"I was free of his hurtful ways, but not of the consequences," Lucy corrected. "The truth is, the two years I spent married to him changed me. It changed who I once was. And now I can never go back."

"Is that what you think I'm doing? Making a mistake that I can never go back from?"

"I don't know. Perhaps no one knows except you and Will and God." She shrugged, wishing she had a better ability to speak about what was in her heart. "I guess I'm just trying to tell you that I have learned that nothing is a simple, singular choice. Our lives are intertwined with each other, like the honeysuckle vines growing on the fence outside. Everything we do affects so many other people, for better or worse. So, perhaps, it is better to live life a little too cautiously than in a headstrong fashion."

In a deliberate manner, Gwen carefully scooped the orange sections into the glass bowl in between them, then rinsed off her knife.

Lucy sliced strawberries and waited. Giving Gwen time to reflect on what she said.

After drying her hands with a dish towel, Gwen faced her. "I want to thank you for telling me about your marriage. I know it couldn't have been easy."

"It wasn't."

"You've given me a lot to think about." She raised her eyes to the ceiling in a winsome way. "I think I, too, have been guilty of not thinking about what a marriage would truly be like. Instead, I've only been thinking of making my mother's and sister's lives easier."

"I didn't mean to change your mind . . . just to make you realize that there are always consequences."

"I understand." She sighed. "Now I want to leave with something for you to think about."

"Yes?"

"In all the time Calvin and I were sweethearts, he never once looked at me the way I've seen him look at you."

Stunned, Lucy shook her head. "I doubt—"

"Don't doubt. I promise. I wouldn't make something like that up."

And before Lucy could ask Gwen what she meant by that remark, Gwen left the kitchen, just as her Aunt Jenna walked in the front door.

"Lucy?" Jenna called out, her voice strained.

Lucy ran to the entryway. Her aunt was standing by the front door, looking pale and exhausted. "Yes?"

"Could you please help me get Mattie inside? I'm afraid it's been a terribly difficult day."

"Of course," Lucy replied.

She followed her aunt outside to the van . . . all thoughts of Gwen and Paul and Calvin pushed aside.

As he ground coffee beans and brewed a fresh pot of coffee, John knew he'd never felt more alone. He felt torn between two worlds, and two choices. Jayne Donovan, and her English life. Her flirty glances, her humor, the way she smiled when she talked and seemed to care about everyone around her. Jayne was the type of woman he used to dream of having a relationship with when he was living on the farm and yearning for the excitement of the big city.

She was polished and beautiful and vibrant.

So much like Angela in some ways, but different, too. John knew Jayne was made of sterner stuff than Angela. She was stronger, more independent. Far less spoiled.

And he'd seen the flash of interest for him in her eyes.

Instinctively, he knew she was waiting for him to ask her out. Waiting for him to call her.

Now that the coffee was brewing, he got to work organizing one of the bakery cases. A bank teller had come in early and bought three dozen donuts for her office. There'd been a line by the time she'd left, and he'd never had a chance to put things to right again.

Kneeling, he arranged the last of the donuts and let his mind drift back to his love life, such that it was.

Of course, Mary came to mind. The widow. The *Amish* widow. Oh, but his heart went out to her. She was trying so hard to take care of her boy. He, being twelve, was pulling away from her as quickly as possible.

Mary seemed to find joy in the simplest of things. She made him yearn to be more gentle, more patient, more giving than he'd ever felt in his entire life. When he was around Mary, he melted—there was no other word for it. She made him want to be a better person, to reach out to others more. To be kinder.

And, of course, he yearned to help her. He wanted to help with Abel. He wanted to be the person she could lean on, because he was coming to realize that Mary needed someone strong in her life, to help bear her burdens.

A pan clanked as he wiped it down and stacked it on the others he'd take into the kitchen later.

Just as the door to the shop opened. He almost cried in relief, especially when he saw who had wandered in. Visiting with his nephew would definitely take his mind off his problems. "Calvin. It's good to see you. What brings you in?" He grabbed a plate. "Hungry?"

"Always." Calvin grinned.

"I'll get you a couple of donuts."

"Thanks." He paused. "Uncle John, the food sounds good, but I mainly just wanted to see you. Do you have time to talk?"

"I have nothing but time. Sit down." Opening up the case, he pulled out a pair of plain cake donuts and poured two mugs full of the fresh-brewed coffee. "How are things? How's my Katie?"

Calvin grimaced. "She tripped playing jump rope and somehow bit her lip. It's swollen and red. Bled something awful."

John tried to find the silver lining. "Perhaps she won't be able to talk for a day or two?"

"We only got two hours' break," his nephew said with a laugh. "I'll bring her in soon so you can admire her split lip. She's terribly proud of it."

"Oh, but your father would have enjoyed your sister's scrapes."

Calvin stilled. "You think so?"

"Of course. He loved a good laugh. And he got in a fair amount of trouble when he was young, too."

"I thought he'd been perfect . . ."

"He was a good man. The best man I knew. But he wasn't perfect, Calvin." He paused. "No one is."

Calvin frowned. "I'm definitely not."

"What happened?"

"I betrayed a woman's trust."

"Lucy's?"

"*Jah.*" He rolled his eyes. "I guess it's obvious, huh?"

"A little."

"Do you think I'm hopeless? I should be able to handle relationships better. Don't you think? At my age?"

John couldn't help laughing. "If the Lord gave us wisdom with age, we'd be in even more of a hurry to grow up! And to get old."

"Are you having problems, too?"

"A little. I'm just trying to figure out where I fit in the world. That's all."

After he finished the cup of coffee, Calvin wiped his mouth and stood up. "Thanks, Onkle."

"Did I help?"

"Definitely."

"I'm glad." Quickly, he went around the corner and pulled out a sack of donut holes. "Give these to Katie, would you? And tell her I hope she feels better."

"I will," Calvin said with a smile, then left.

John crossed his arms over his chest and tried to imagine what his life would be like if he was Amish again. If he was Amish, he could court Mary. Her sweet smile would surely make every day fresh and perfect.

But would he fit in again? Or would he still be standing on the outskirts, wanting other things?

Was someone like Jayne better suited to him? After all, she'd survived a divorce, too. And she was a caring, lovely woman—proving that it wasn't just Amish women who reached out to others.

But if he chose Jayne, what would happen to Mary's boy? Already, he felt something for him. And John had thought Mary had stopped by more frequently now.

There was definitely something between them—proving that desire and sparks were alive and well in the Amish community, too.

He sighed. What was he doing, anyway? It wasn't like either woman was tapping her foot, waiting for a marriage proposal.

It just . . . felt like a decision needed to be made. He hoped the good Lord would give him some guidance sooner than later.

Chapter 26

"So, your time in our little town is coming to a close, I hear?" Calvin asked as they walked along the path between their two houses. The day was almost warm, not too hot or humid. Honeysuckle bloomed in thickets around them, permeating the air with their sweet smell.

"*Jah*. I've been here a whole month now. It's time to go home." She attempted to smile, but it was difficult. So much had changed in just one month's time. When she'd first arrived, the ground had been damp from the rains and many flowers were just popping up from the ground. Now there was a riot of color surrounding them; vivid shades of pinks and yellows and reds greeted them wherever they looked.

She'd also changed. And, just like the flowers, she had bloomed. Lucy knew she was no longer the same person she was on the train. She'd become stronger inside. More self-assured.

And because of that, she felt her usual reticence had diminished and she was more able to speak with other people. It was easier to smile. To laugh. To come out of her shell.

To hold her head up high.

"It's time that I got out of Aunt Jenna's kitchen. Hardly a day passes when I'm not in her way," Lucy quipped.

"I doubt she has minded your help. Although perhaps not your mess?"

Enjoying his teasing, she added, "I have a feeling Mattie might feel relieved to see me on my way as well. I've been fussing over her something awful, practically talking her ear off. And, well, you know the saying about houseguests . . ."

"What, that they go bad after a few days? That wasn't you, Lucy." Darting forward, he held up a branch so she could step under it as they continued down the windy dirt path. "I'm sure Mattie has been grateful for all of your help. Your being here did make a difference."

"I hope so. I tried my best."

"I know so. Actually, I've heard she's enjoyed your visit *verra* much."

"I've enjoyed being with her, too. I just wish I had been able to make things better."

"Lucy, you can't take the blame for not curing Mattie's cancer."

She smiled. Calvin was right, though it made no sense. A time or two she had stayed up during the evening, blaming herself for that very thing. "I didn't mean to take the blame, but sometimes I fear I did." Then, thinking about why she was like that, she added, "It's a habit of mine."

He stopped. "Because of your husband?"

Well, here it was. She either had to take a chance and reach out to Calvin, and tell him all her truths, or push them away into the dark place where they'd dwell . . . and hope that they wouldn't surface again.

"Yes. Because of Paul. When we were married, I felt myself taking the blame for a lot of things," she said. "Somehow, I began to believe him when he constantly said I wasn't good enough."

"He was a cruel man, Lucy."

"At first I didn't think so. At first I thought he just had a terrible temper."

"Which is why you were worried about mine?"

"Yes." Though her insides were quaking, Lucy pushed herself. She could do this. She could talk about her past in a strong way. In a way that would illustrate how far she'd come. "Calvin, I lived with him for two years. During that time, I started doing whatever I could to survive. Even if it meant I pretended it was only his temper that drove him to hit me."

He stilled. "Lucy, I don't know if I'll ever be able to think of that man as anything but evil. I hate to think of him hurting you so. Of abusing you so."

Abused. It was such a harsh word. So many people in her life had glossed over it, choosing to say instead that Paul had difficulties with his temper.

But now she knew that abuse came in many forms. It didn't just happen in one way, or for one reason. No, the abuser made a decision to be that way, long before any words were said or pain was inflicted. Nothing she could have done back then would have made Paul act differently. And nothing she could say now would erase the pain—and the images from her mind.

She finally replied. "Soon after we married, Paul got mad at me and slammed me against our bedroom wall." Keeping her eyes averted so she wouldn't see the dismay in his eyes, Lucy continued: "The next morning, he cried and apologized. And I vowed to try to be a better wife. But I soon learned that I was never going to be good enough."

Finally she lifted her head and steeled herself to see his reaction. She'd learned that sometimes people didn't understand why she stayed.

They didn't understand what it was like to feel like there was nowhere else to go.

But instead of scorn, Calvin's eyes filled with tears. "I'm so sorry," he murmured. "I'm so terribly sorry, Lucy."

"It wasn't your fault."

"Lucy, I am so sorry for you." His voice turning grim, he shook his head. "And I am sorry for the things that I am thinking, too."

"What?"

"I fear that if that man was in front of me right now, I'd be tempted to give him a taste of his own medicine."

"Oh, Calvin." Though the conversation was so hard, his fierce words made her smile.

"I know I shouldn't want violence. But I hate the idea of you having lived like that."

She bit her lip. What could she say? "It was a horrible

way to live. I felt trapped." Remembering the things she wrote in her journal, she swallowed hard.

"I know you did."

When their eyes met, the words she'd written in her journal flashed in her mind. "Calvin, what you saw, what you read . . . it was just words, you know?" Before he could say a word, she rushed on. "I promise, I didn't want him to die. I didn't celebrate it. Those things I wrote . . ." Feeling inadequate, she let her voice drift off.

"Everyone has private thoughts they aren't proud of. I was the one at fault, not you."

"Will you ever be able to forget what I wrote? I . . . I would hate for you to think the worst of me."

He stilled. "I don't."

When he didn't add anything, Lucy steeled her spine. Instinctively, she knew that she was never going to be able to move on if she didn't finally tell someone the whole, awful truth. "When I cried for him . . . it was tears of relief. It was very hard, living in fear."

"I would have felt the same way," he said after a moment. "I'm glad you didn't mourn him."

With his words, a huge weight lifted off her shoulders. At least he understood.

When they got to the blackberry vines, Calvin plucked one and immediately popped it into his mouth. Lucy did the same, enjoying the sweet, tart juice. After Calvin had eaten two more, he pulled another four berries and deposited them in her pail.

"Lucy, it just occurred to me that you were a caregiver then, too."

"What do you mean?"

"I mean, you did your best to shield your family from worry. You didn't want your sisters to worry over you. Or your parents to feel that burden of guilt."

"I'm the oldest. They shouldn't worry about me."

"You're one of the most selfless people I've ever met, Lucy Troyer."

"No. Just someone who was trying to survive."

"Perhaps more than that?"

"Like I said, Calvin. It is over now. It doesn't really matter. I just wanted you to know the whole truth about my marriage. About why I don't speak of him much. And about why I don't grieve for my husband as much as other widows."

He took a deep breath. "And now I understand, too, why you acted the way you did outside the train station in Toledo."

Thinking back to the turn of her thoughts, Lucy wondered how she could have so misjudged him. "All I heard when you yelled was Paul. I wasn't even thinking that you weren't out of control, or that you were simply trying to help the horse. All I saw was a man who could get angry."

"And so you ran."

"I ran. I wish now that I hadn't. I wish that I had trusted you more."

"It's okay now, don'tcha think?"

"It is okay now."

As the sun rose above them, and its warm rays heated their skin, Lucy relaxed. At last, Calvin understood. And though he might always have questions about her past, at least now he could understand why she was the way she was. And that was worth much to her.

But there was one more thing that lay between them: Gwen.

"Are you still upset with Gwen and Will?"

"No. We ended up talking, and I talked with Will, too. The Lord was really at work with the three of us, I'll tell you that. Left to our own devices, we might have all ended up bitter and miserable with each other."

"What led you to the discussion?"

"You, as a matter of fact."

"Me?" She couldn't have been more surprised. "I didn't do anything."

"You're right. You did *everything*. Lucy, you showed me what it was like to give of yourself instead of take. You helped me understand that sometimes what we want isn't what we should get. And because of your example, I learned to accept that." He paused, then blurted, "Lucy, I care about you. I care about you a lot."

She smiled, feeling like her whole being was glowing from his words. "I feel the same way."

"Are you sure you can't stay longer?"

"I wish I could, but I can't. My parents asked me to help with the little ones so they can go to a wedding. I promised them they could count on me." Lucy looked at him, silently asking him to give her a reason to stay. Waited for him to offer to visit her.

"All right, then," he said with a sigh. "I guess we can still write to each other . . ."

"Yes. I'll write to you often."

His mouth opened, just like he had something very important to say. But just as quickly, he closed it again.

A moment passed. "Well," he finally said awkwardly. "I guess we'll just have to make the most of today, hmm?"

Her heart deflated, but she did her best to try to be positive. They'd had enough dark and sad conversations for a lifetime. "That's a good plan."

He held out a hand. "Want to walk a bit more?"

"Sure."

But instead of taking her hand, he wrapped an arm around her shoulders and pressed his lips to her brow. Helping her feel at peace. And very, very cherished.

Later that afternoon, when they were just steps from Mattie's house, Calvin pulled her into a fierce embrace. "I'm going to miss you," he murmured. "I'm going to miss you very much."

Closing her eyes, Lucy leaned into him. With all her heart, she hoped she would never forget this moment. Never forget feeling treasured and wanted and cared for.

For about the twentieth time that night, Lucy glanced at the clock ticking too loudly on Mattie's dresser. It was after nine now. Late.

In less than an hour, John Weaver would be by. He'd very kindly offered to drive her to the train station so she could stay as long as possible with Mattie.

Wearily, Lucy brushed a cool cloth over Mattie's brow and continued to pray for her cousin. Mattie flinched from the compress but otherwise lay motionless.

Lucy closed her eyes and willed the tears not to fall.

Crying wouldn't help anything, and would only upset Mattie.

But, oh, it was hard.

"I'm so tired of being this way, Lucy," Mattie said after a while. "I'm so tired of being so weak."

"I know." Hoping she sounded more optimistic than she felt, Lucy said, "Your doctors said you are almost done with the worst of it."

"I doubt it. Sometimes I think they say those things just to keep my hopes up."

Privately, she wondered if that was true. Mattie was so terribly sick and weak.

Then again, perhaps there wasn't anything wrong with the doctors and the rest of the medical staff trying to keep up the optimism.

Lately, Mattie had been in a dark place and had refused to pray with her. "The doctors aren't in the business of telling people what they want to hear," she said briskly. "They have to concentrate on the facts."

"Well, *my* fact is that this chemotherapy is making me terribly ill, indeed," Mattie pronounced, her voice sounding hollow, almost lifeless. After another heartbeat, she closed her eyes. "Maybe I shouldn't have let them treat me."

"What are you saying?" Feeling at a complete loss, Lucy grew frantic. "Of course you needed treatment! That's the only way to get better."

"I'm not feelin' so much better now."

"But you will."

"I don't know." Mattie sighed, her eyes still closed. "Lucy, I feel bad. Really bad."

Lucy's hands shook as she dipped the cloth into the cool water again. "I know."

"I—I don't want to do this much longer." Her eyes opened, revealing dilated pupils. "Lucy, perhaps the medicine isn't working."

Injecting steel into her voice, Lucy shook her head. "Come now, Mattie. Please try and think more positively. This medicine is working. You and I both know it—and the nurses and doctors said it, too. Soon, this difficult time will pass. We both know that difficult things are only sweet after hardship."

"You can say that. But has anything really improved with you?" she asked bitterly. "You are still hurting. You're still afraid to move forward."

Lucy pushed down her hurt. Mattie was not being herself. She wasn't meaning to be so cruel.

"I've found peace," Lucy said finally. "I've found strength. Both come from the knowledge that the Lord has been by my side, guiding me."

After a moment, Mattie spoke: "I think He left me."

Lucy was confused. "Who, dear? Who left you?"

"God."

"Oh, Mattie! Don't say that. God would never leave you."

"I can't help it. It's how I feel. I feel that if He loved me like we were taught that He does, He wouldn't be making me suffer so."

"Stop that talk."

Mattie blinked, then smiled weakly. "What happened to your patience? What happened to the best caregiver

I've ever had? Where's the woman who has been so angelic? Who's been praying and working and smiling . . . who's been constantly saying the right thing?"

"My cousin has used up my supply of patience," Lucy snapped.

Meeting her gaze, the spark in Mattie's dark brown eyes faded again. "Then we're both in a world of hurt," she said, her voice flat.

Scooting closer, she slid a hand along Mattie's soft quilt and gripped her hand. "Listen. You must get better. And you must believe that you can."

"Why?"

"Because that's your job."

"Lucy—"

Desperate times called for desperate words. "Mattie, if I can survive two years with Paul, you can certainly survive this."

Her cousin's eyes widened. "I can't believe you said that. I've never heard you speak of your life with Paul as 'surviving.' "

"Maybe you never needed to hear those words before. But I promise you that's how I feel. Living is sometimes easy, Mattie. But surviving . . . surviving is the difficult thing. And that is what makes you grow and become strong." Leaning close, she murmured, "Don't you dare give up."

"But, Lucy—"

Lucy shook her head. "Don't say it. You need to find the strength and start fighting. Be a survivor, Mattie," she urged. "Be a survivor, not a victim." Minutes passed as they stared at each other in silence so sharp and tense it felt like a tangible thing.

Then finally . . . finally Mattie nodded. "All right."

Lucy sighed in relief. "Thank the good Lord."

After a bit, Mattie clutched her hand. "Hey, Luce?"

"Yes, dear?"

"Is there any way you can stay here longer?"

Lucy shook her head with regret. As much as she wanted to be there for her cousin, she knew it was time to go home. "I'm afraid not. I promised my *mamm* that I'd come home and help with the little ones. She's counting on me. I can't let her down."

"No, you can't." Her lip trembled. With effort, Mattie controlled herself. "I suppose we're all counting on you, Lucy. You must be careful, or we'll all take and take . . . until you have nothing left."

"That won't ever happen. God is with me, and He will help me. Just as He will help you, if you open your heart again."

For one split second, Mattie met her gaze, and all the love that they held for each other passed between them. For one split second, Lucy felt as if they were as close as they ever were.

As close as they'd be, if they were truly sisters.

But then Mattie looked away and closed her eyes. "I'm so, so tired."

"You should try to sleep."

"I don't want to sleep until you leave."

As if on cue, Jenna poked her head into the room. "Lucy, John Weaver is here. It's time for you to go."

Gently, Lucy pulled her hand away from Mattie's and reluctantly got to her feet. "All right. I'll be right out."

Turning to Mattie, she whispered, "I will be writing you and checking up on you, too. And I will be praying for you as well. Enough for the two of us."

Though Mattie said nothing, she swallowed hard.

"Mattie, do you understand?"

"I do," she finally replied. "But there's no need."

"You did it for me," Lucy coaxed. "You prayed for me when I needed it. When I needed the prayers but had no strength, you prayed enough for two. Now it's my turn. I will pray for you and me, Mattie. And I will keep praying, as long as it takes. I promise you this."

Quickly, before she burst into tears, she bent down and kissed Mattie's brow. Then, after brief hugs to her aunt and uncle, she ran out the door and to John, who was loading her bag in the back of his truck.

"Hi, Lucy," John said gently. "You ready to get back to your own home?"

"Oh, yes," she murmured, doing her best to sound cheerful.

But inside she was wondering what in the world she was going to do. She'd done her best. Everything she possibly could. But the reality was that she'd tried her best and failed.

In many ways, she'd failed as a caregiver. And that knowledge almost broke her heart.

Chapter 27

It was storming. As water spattered against the window next to her seat, Lucy leaned back against the cushion and watched the thick drops fall. Somehow it seemed fitting that the rain had come again, she supposed. She'd come full circle.

For almost the whole month she'd been in Jacob's Crossing, nary a drop had fallen. It had been so dry that many of the farmers said the unusual weather might have damaged their crops.

She, on the other hand, had enjoyed every single moment of the bright sunshine. The warm rays heating her face gave her hope, reminding her that with patience, all things come when they are supposed to. Now that Mattie's weeks of chemotherapy were almost over, Lucy hoped with all her heart that she would soon recover completely. Perhaps if her body grew more healthy and strong, Mattie's spirit would improve, too. Nothing would make Lucy happier than to see her cousin become more like her old self.

But until then, she would keep praying for Mattie. Pray for her healing and for her heart and soul. She would pray enough for two.

She was going to pray for herself, too. Right then and there, she vowed that she would pray more and write a little less in her journal. While putting all her emotions on paper had helped, seeking guidance and God's love would help even more.

And hopefully, before too long, the Lord would help her figure out her future with Calvin.

Calvin.

She'd fought with him, and fought her own tumultuous feelings about love and marriage and relationships again and again. Little by little, she'd opened her heart to him. Lucy still was amazed that she'd told him so many of her darkest worries and secrets. Before Calvin, she'd planned to keep it all deep inside of herself. She'd been so sure that if she shared everything in her past, she would frighten another person away.

But instead of being frightened, Calvin had acted like she'd given him a challenge instead. Time and again he'd met her challenges. And had made her challenge herself, too.

Such as when he'd lost his temper and she'd pushed him away before he'd had a chance to explain himself. And when she'd realized that even if Calvin wasn't perfect, he'd never be like Paul.

No, Calvin would never be the type of man who enjoyed hurting women.

As rain continued to splatter against the pane, and the other train passengers continued to board, Lucy looked at all of them, sometimes nodding in recognition of their inquisitive stares or hesitant smiles.

Sometimes smiling right back.

Oh, my, but what a difference a month had made! Her journey east had been filled with doubts and worries. The whole time, she'd been afraid and insecure. Doubting herself. Doubting her ability to make a difference with Mattie.

She'd been so worried about the rain, and about the weather, and about the lights turning off and on. And, then, of course, God had handed over her worst fears and had forced her to confront them.

And, just like always, she had found He had given her the tools not only to survive but to come through stronger than before.

As drops of rain beaded on the window, then dripped down the glass, Lucy shook her head in wonder. When was she ever going to learn that she was stronger than she thought? When was she ever going to remember that with God, all things are possible?

Even in her darkest hours?

"Excuse me, it looks like I'm your seat mate."

The voice was warm and masculine. Her heart lurched as she looked up, half expecting to see the man who'd occupied all her dreams.

But it wasn't Calvin, of course.

Now that he had her attention, the *Englischer* spoke again. "Hi. You, uh, might want to watch your dress. I'm afraid every part of me is soaking wet." He rolled his eyes as the faint flush of happiness colored his cheeks. "My girlfriend was reluctant to let me go."

His awkwardness was charming. And it was enough to shake off the cobwebs and make room for him. "Oh. Yes. Of course. Here, let me move over a bit." She shifted about a little, taking care to keep her skirts neatly folded around her as the man, who was about her age, sat down.

"Thanks." He smiled. "So, where are you off to?"

"I'm going home. To Michigan."

"I'm headed to Chicago." He grinned. "I guess we'll be sitting near each other for hours."

She held up the book in her lap. "I bought a book for the trip."

"I wasn't nearly that organized. But I'm planning to sleep, anyway. I'm exhausted. Wake me up if I start snoring, would you?"

"Of course," she murmured.

As the train pulled out and the lights dimmed, Lucy settled herself again. Next to her, the man sprawled out and promptly fell asleep.

As a hint of a snore escaped his lips, Lucy couldn't resist smiling. He certainly hadn't been kidding about falling asleep. But though he was indeed snoring, she wouldn't wake him up. He was lucky to be able to sleep so easily.

Which, again, brought her mind back to the earlier trip.

No matter how hard she'd tried, she certainly hadn't been able to sleep when Calvin had been near! No, she'd been too aware of him. And by the topsy-turvy mixture of emotions he provoked. All just by sitting down by her side.

Lucy folded her hands neatly in her lap and attempted to think of something to do. But the hour was late, and neither reading nor crochet held any appeal. So she closed her eyes and daydreamed, remembered how warm the sun had felt on her face. Finally, she dozed.

And the dreams came again.

She was walking on a windy dirt path. Golden honeysuckle surrounded her, making the air fragrant. Making the path beautiful.

"Lucy!" a man called out to her. Startling her.

She began to run.

The voice came again. "Lucy! Lucy, stop!"

He was coming closer. She picked up her pace. Her chest burned as she gasped for air, pulled oxygen into her lungs. Dirt turned to dust, flying in the air, clouding her path.

Panic gripped her hard. Just as a hand reached out and grabbed her elbow. With a jerk, she turned her head. Steeled herself to see him.

But all she heard was a whistle.

Lucy gasped, filling her lungs with air—prepared to cry out . . . and then she heard the train whistle blow again.

"Toledo!" a voice rang out. Two people stood up and walked down the aisle.

To her surprise, the *Englischer* who'd been by her side was nowhere to be found. Because the overhead lights were on, Lucy looked around with interest. Another person left. Two others took vacant seats.

"I'm sorry, is this seat taken?"

She looked up in surprise. "Yes, it's—"

"Me," Calvin Weaver said.

"You!" She scrambled to her feet and reached for his hand. "Calvin? Whatever are you doing here?" To her pleasure, his fingers curved around hers instantly.

"Riding on the train. So, Lucy, is this seat taken?"

"I think so. By a man going to Chicago." Craning her neck, she saw no sign of him. "I'm not sure where he is, though."

"No worries. I'll put my things in this seat here." After he set down that orange backpack that she'd recognize anywhere, he scanned the aisles. Lucy watched as most of the people in the seats stared at him.

Abruptly, he turned to her. "You know what? Why don't we go somewhere else? Would you like to take a walk with me? This train has a viewing car."

At the moment, she felt like she'd follow him anywhere. "Sure," she sputtered.

As the whistle blew and the train pulled forward out of the Toledo station, Calvin reached for her hand. Lucy held on tightly as she followed him down the rocking aisle and through the narrow passage that connected the train cars.

When they were in the viewing car, Calvin led her to a spot on the far left, where no one else was. She settled herself next to him, breathed in his scent, and finally asked the question that had been burning inside her. "Why are you here?"

"Because I couldn't stay away."

He sounded so sure. So confident. So like himself! Her

heart started beating faster as she tried to think of the right response.

"Lucy, I know it's hardly been a day, but I missed you terribly. The moment you left, I realized I had been wrong to let you go." Taking one of her hands, he smiled gently. "Lucy, do you remember our last conversation?"

She nodded.

He continued. "We said some terribly important things. Things that matter to us. That mattered to me, deeply."

"They mattered to me, too," she sputtered. Of course she remembered.

"But as soon as you left, I realized that though we said many important things, I had neglected to tell you the most important thing of all." He reached for her hand. "I forgot to tell you that I love you."

Her insides melted at his words—and how could they not? Calvin's words were every dream she'd hoped would come true.

But it felt so sudden. After all, they'd known each other only a month. And for much of that time, they'd been struggling with secrets.

"This is crazy!" she said with a laugh. "Calvin, we promised to write—"

"I didn't want to wait that long. The fact is, once I knew how I felt—without a doubt—I ran to catch this train."

"This train?" she clarified. When he nodded, she blurted, "Calvin Weaver, you've been on this train with me the whole time?"

"I have."

"Why didn't you find me earlier?"

"Because I've been trying to find the courage to face you."

Calvin Weaver, the most confident man she'd ever met, had been nervous about seeing her? "I can't imagine that."

"Oh, imagine it, Lucy," he said drily. "I've been sitting in my seat, trying to come up with the right words to tell you how I feel. But none of them worked. None of them were good enough. None were perfect."

"But I don't need perfect words."

He smiled. "I'm glad, because even after practicing for an hour, I still don't have them." With care, he took her other hand and linked their fingers. Rubbed one thumb over the fine bones of her hand. Carefully, she realized. As if he would never wish to do her harm.

"Lucy, all I do know is that you've become so special to me. I want you in my life, by my side."

Wordlessly, she stared back at him. The words he was saying were so special, shattering all her memories of Paul. Taking a deep breath, he spoke again. "Lucy, I want to marry you. I want you to come live with me in Jacob's Crossing."

Her chest felt so tight, Lucy felt as if all the air had been pushed out of her.

Mistaking her silence for confusion, a shadow of worry entered his eyes. His speech quickened. "I know you've been hurt in the past. And though I've said this before, I'll say it as many times as you need to hear it. Lucy, I will never lay a hand on you. I never want to make you cry. I promise. My only goal will be to make you happy."

Sitting there, their hands linked, her heart beating so

loudly she felt the world could hear it, Lucy believed him. Now she trusted him. Trusted him enough to realize he would only care for her. That he wanted to be her partner, not her superior. "Calvin, I know you will make me happy," she said simply. Because, really, nothing else seemed to matter. She trusted Calvin like she'd never trusted anyone else in her life. And she longed to be with him, like she'd never wanted another man before.

Again, his expression filled with doubt. And resolve. "Lucy, if you'll give us a chance, I'll follow your lead. We can take things as slow as you want. We can be engaged for as long as you'd like. For as long as it will take for you to trust me. To trust us. I mean . . . that is . . . if you decide you want me, too."

Lucy smiled. "I do, Calvin Weaver."

"You do . . . what? You do want me . . . ?"

"I do want to marry you," she said, feeling so sure. So happy—perhaps feeling the happiest she'd ever felt in her life. God had just given her a gift. A gift of love and a happy future. She felt His approval. And His love for her . . . and for Calvin. "Calvin, I do not need a long time to know that my heart will be safe with you."

The pure joy that lit his eyes made her smile. "You've made me terribly happy."

"I feel the same way." As they stared at each other, there in the near-empty train car, Lucy couldn't help but feel giddy. Words could never convey what she was feeling.

But perhaps they didn't need to?

"Are you sure you won't mind leaving Michigan?" Calvin asked.

"I wouldn't mind at all. I want to start over," she said. "I want to start over someplace where I only have happy memories, where the two of us can plan a future together. I can't think of a better place to do that than in Jacob's Crossing."

Calvin squeezed her hands. Exhaled. Almost looked content.

Almost. His gaze drifted to her lips. Almost as swiftly, he looked away. Suddenly shy.

Lucy realized he wasn't going to kiss her or even hug her without her permission. He was too afraid of spooking her. Of pushing.

But now that she knew what love was, Lucy realized she had no fears at all. A quick inspection revealed that they were still alone in the train car. As alone as they were ever going to be for the next many hours.

She leaned a little closer. "Calvin, perhaps you'd like to kiss me?"

One of his palms released her own and cradled her jaw. Unable to help herself, she pressed her cheek against his hand, enjoying the feel of his hand on her skin.

"You wouldn't mind?"

"Not at all." She bit her lip, then continued: "I want to kiss you. I mean, if that . . . if that is what you want—"

She wasn't able to finish because his lips were on hers then. Tenderly kissing her. Tenderly making her feel loved.

Caring for her. Just as she'd cared for him. Little by little, she leaned closer. Rested her palms on his shoulders. Calvin's hands skimmed her arms, then lightly closed around her back. After too short a time, he broke away.

Lucy felt a shiver run through her. Everything with Calvin was so perfect. So sweet. So worth waiting for.

He looked into her eyes and smiled. "Lucy, when I stopped being afraid to give you my heart, I realized something."

"And what is that?"

"My heart wasn't in jeopardy with you at all. Instead of being hurt, it would be cared for. By you."

"Always," Lucy said. "I will always care for you."

As they sat together, side by side on the train, Lucy knew that she could finally look forward to the idea of always. Of Always . . . And Forever.

At last.

Dear Reader,

I was on a cruise when I learned I had a new contract with Avon Inspire. How neat was that? I was thrilled. I celebrated! I love writing, and was I very excited to get home and start on a new series.

However, God had other plans. When we got off the ship and were in the Ft. Lauderdale airport, I checked our home messages and discovered my mother was in the hospital. She'd been having some heart problems and was disoriented.

Suddenly, everything I thought mattered so much didn't matter so much at all.

Over the next few weeks, I flew to California, spoke to doctors, and called my brother and sister more than I'd called them in years. Our mom would get better, things would settle down, then one of us would get another phone call and find out she was in the emergency room again. It was a frustrating and very hard time.

Yet, it was also an incredibly meaningful time. I discovered that my siblings and I still had a strong bond that not even years spent living thousands of miles apart could break.

During all of this, I began writing *The Caregiver.*

Now, looking back on those weeks, I have to smile. It was so obvious that God was right there with me! He helped me craft what I'd originally planned to be a somewhat light, upbeat story into a novel far more meaningful.

He helped me with Lucy's character, too, as I imagined what kind of a woman would leave her family, travel to another state, and volunteer to care for someone going through chemotherapy. At first, I was sure that woman would have to be an independent, incredibly strong woman.

But then I started thinking about Lucy some more. I started asking questions, too. What if she wasn't very strong? Or even better, what if she was stronger than she ever imagined she was? A woman like that, I decided, would make a great heroine. A woman like that was Lucy Troyer.

I hope you enjoyed Lucy's journey to Jacob's Crossing, her romance with Calvin Weaver, and her calling to become the type of person she was meant to be.

I hope you'll continue with the series as the people of Jacob's Crossing have even more adventures. I promise, Calvin's Uncle John is about to go on quite an emotional roller coaster, as does the rest of the Weaver family. Even little five-year-old Katie has some growing pains!

Finally, if you've ever smiled at the grocery-store clerk when you were sad, happily volunteered when you really wanted to cry, or said you were "just fine" when maybe you weren't "just fine" at all . . . this book is for you. God bless you.

With my thanks,

Shelley Shepard Gray

PS: To everyone who's asked your library to carry my books, thank you! To all the librarians who've recommended my novels and asked me to speak at their libraries, thank you, too. I'm really looking forward to visiting and meeting your patrons.

In the meantime, please visit me at www.shelleyshepardgray.com or on Facebook, or write to me at: Shelley Shepard Gray, 10663 Loveland-Madeira Rd. #167, Loveland, Ohio 45140. I'd truly love to hear what you thought of the book.

Discussion Questions

1. Lucy and Calvin are on the train to Cleveland by chance. However, that one coincidence changes their lives in numerous ways. Can you think of an experience in your life when a "chance" meeting led to a lifelong friendship?

2. Calvin's personality is far different from Lucy's. While she's reserved, he's outgoing. Where she is timid, he is sometimes too gregarious. Do you think they really were a good match? What qualities did Lucy and Calvin each bring to their relationship that the other lacked?

3. After twenty years, John Weaver returns to Jacob's Crossing. He hopes to reconnect with his extended family. John's story continues through the next two

books in the series. What do you think will happen to him? Can you ever really go home again?

4. Do you think John will stay in Jacob's Crossing? Already, he's interested in two different women, Jayne and Mary. Do you think either woman will be the right partner for him?

5. While Mattie Lapp endures chemotherapy, she's struggling with her faith and depression. Was there a time in your life when you also experienced a crisis of faith? If so, what helped you cope?

6. Was Lucy the "right" person to be Mattie's caregiver? Why or why not?

7. As I wrote about Lucy, I often thought she was one of the strongest heroines I've ever created. She survived years of abuse and the death of a spouse and was able to still reach out to others. Is there anyone in your life who has displayed a great strength that you admire?

8. *Happiness is the inner joy that can be sought or caught, but never taught or bought.*

From the moment I read this Amish proverb, I knew it was the perfect quotation to start my novel. How can this proverb about happiness be applied to your life?

9. *Even when I walk through the darkest valley, I will not be afraid, for you are close beside me* ~Psalm 23:4

God is present with all of the characters in this novel. Lucy knows that without her faith, she could never have survived her marriage to Paul. Calvin and John's faith gave them a positive outlook for their future. Finally, God has blessed Mattie with a loving family, a giving community, and a good friend in Graham—all people who want to help make her recovery easier. When has God's presence helped you through a difficult time?

Don't miss Shelley Shepard Gray's next
book in the Families of Honor series,

The Protector

On sale summer 2011

No matter how hard she tried, Ella Hostetler found it almost impossible to look away from the white canvas tent that covered the majority of her front yard.

She swallowed hard. Ah, it wasn't even *her* yard anymore. It, along with the house, barn, and most of the belongings inside, now belonged to other people.

Now she had practically nothing.

"Ella, please don't stand and stare any longer. Watching you makes my heart break," Corrine said, her voice turning more troubled by the second. "Ach, but I knew I should have made you come over to my house today."

Corrine was a good friend. Her best friend in the world, next to Dorothy. But even good friends couldn't make difficult things go away. "I had to be here," Ella said. "Someone had to stay in case anyone bidding had a question." She tried to smile. "And it's not like there was anyone else to take my place."

Pure dismay entered Corrine's eyes. "Oh, but you've had such a time of it. First your father passed away, and then you had to spend all your time nursing your mother and taking care of the house. By yourself."

"I *am* an only child, Corrine."

"I know. But sometimes I just feel so badly for you, having to sell everything."

Privately, Ella felt bad for herself, too. But hearing the

doom and gloom in her girlfriend's voice pushed her to try to sound positive. "It will be a relief to not have so much to take care of," Ella said, almost believing it to be true. "And the money earned today will guarantee my future."

"Oh, Ella. You sound like you will never marry. You will."

"Maybe. Or maybe not. Perhaps I'll just be like Dorothy. She seems to be doing fine on her own."

Something flickered in her best friend's eyes. Was it distaste? Or distrust? "You are not like Dorothy. I've never met a crustier woman."

"She's not so bad."

"She's difficult and bitter. I wish you could have found a different person to move next to."

"The other half of her duplex was empty. Plus, she's excited for me to live there. We're going to work together at the library, you know."

"I know." Corrine pursed her lips. "I just can't help but feel that you're about to lock yourself away from everyone all over again, Ella. You should be making plans to see more people. To laugh a little. Not work and live next to Dorothy Zook."

Another burst of the gavel sang through the air. Preventing Ella from commenting on that.

Casting another worried look her way, Corrine looped her arm through Ella's and pulled. "Come on. Let's go sit down."

Though Ella let herself be led away from the last of the crowd, she couldn't help but look over her shoulder. The knot in her throat expanded, making it almost too hard to talk. "I had no idea I had so many things."

"We all have more than we need, *jah?*"

Ella flinched. Corrine's words were true . . . to a point. She'd known auctioning off her family's farm would be difficult. But this was so much more than that.

First her land and the buildings on it had been bought. And now so many others were picking through and choosing what remained of her parents' lives . . . putting a value on items that to her mother had been priceless.

Her feet slowed as she couldn't resist looking over her shoulder again. Against her will, tears sprang to her eyes as she watched the auctioneer point to her mother's pie safe.

Corrine paused, too. Bit her lip as the auctioneer called out a price. "Ella, what is important are the memories. That is what everyone says."

"I know," she murmured, turning away. It was their way to auction off things of the dead. She understood the meaning behind it—and the far more practical reasoning: She was not going to need most of these items when she lived in town.

But if only memories were what counted, why was everyone else so eager to snatch up her belongings?

"Like I said, it has to be almost over. After all, Loyal Weaver bought most everything when he bought the land."

"Yes, he did." Almost everything that had been her parents' was his now. To her dismay, he'd even bought a lot of the furniture. And her horse and buggy.

One day she would surely be thankful for the money in

her bank account instead of her mare's sweet disposition. One day.

Picking up the pace, they moved farther from the tent. Away from the line of horses and buggies and *Englischers'* cars and trucks.

Away from the life Ella had always known.

They stopped in front of a finely carved bench. Made of weathered oak, the grain had long since been worn to a buttery smooth surface. There was a slight indention near the back, and a nick on the seat, where Ella's father had once foolishly decided to test out his new whittling knife.

"Is right here okay?" Corrine asked.

"It is fine." Yes, it was almost far enough away. As she scanned the crowd through her glasses, most everyone became a blur. And then she saw Loyal Weaver. The man who'd changed her life.

Though it wasn't entirely fair, Ella focused all her pain on him. He was the one who'd been the first to arrive. Who had bid on her things with a gleam in his eye. Who had so much money that he'd paid cash for the land.

Just as if he bought other people's lives all the time.

"I've always liked this bench, Ella," Corrine murmured, claiming her attention again. "Remember how our legs used to swing when we sat here?"

"I remember." The worn bench had many special memories. It had been her grandmother's favorite place to sit on spring mornings. Ella's mother had liked to sit and watch the geese fly south for the winter every October.

Ella herself had perched impatiently on it when she'd

been looking for the English school bus to stop and pick her up.

And now it was Loyal Weaver's. And he most likely didn't even appreciate a bit of what he had.

When the auction was over and the majority of the crowd dispersed, Loyal bit his lip as he watched his older brother, Calvin, walk through the ancient barn. Calvin seemed to catch hold of every flaw in the structure, every crack in the wood. The longer he walked, the deeper his brother's scowl.

After they'd made their way past the stalls and into a pair of rundown, musty tack rooms, Calvin stopped.

"Well?" Loyal asked. There was no sense in beating around the bush. His older brother was nothing if not honest. "What did you think?"

"I think it's terrible."

"Really?" He'd expected some criticism, but not this blunt statement.

"Loyal, it boggles my mind why you bought this place. I don't want to offend, but, really, there's no other way to say it. This place is fallin' apart. Whatever the termites haven't gotten, a good, strong wind will surely blow over."

So much for Calvin not wanting to offend! "This barn ain't so bad."

"It's not so good." After looking around again, Calvin strode out of the tack room. "Being in there makes me think of rats."

"I didn't see more than two," Loyal said drily.

"I'm not laughing, *bruder.*" Crossing the dusty, bug-infested ground, Calvin knocked on the wood of one of the stalls. "My word. This here wood sounds completely rotten."

That would be because it most likely was. "It only needs a little bit of work."

"For every day the rest of your life." His brother pursed his lips, then finally sighed. "I just don't understand why this place, and why now. I know you've been wanting to have a place of your own, but I think you were too hasty. Everything here—the barn, the house, even the land—has been neglected for far too long."

"It has promise." Irritation coursed through him as he crossed the expanse to where his brother stood tapping the toe of his boot like he had somewhere else he'd rather be. "I'm not afraid of hard work, you know." When Calvin's eyes flashed, Loyal braced himself for the next barrage of criticism that was sure to come. "What has you so upset? Are you upset about the money I spent? We agreed it was mine to use how I chose."

"Of course it was your money. And it's not that."

"Then what?" Loyal eyed Calvin, wondering what was going through his brain. Now that he was happily married, had he become complacent? Had he forgotten what it was like to want something of your very own to treasure? To make a mark on?

His brother didn't disappoint. "I know you're not afraid of hard work. And I understand your need to carve out a place all your own. But this place is no good. The barn is in disrepair, the fields are poorly maintained, and that house . . ." He shook his head. "That house is almost worthless. There's nothing of value there."

Loyal thought differently. The Hostetlers' land was on fertile soil and had the makings of a mighty nice farm, indeed. All it had lacked were funds and muscle to make repairs and improvements. He had plenty of both.

The former owners had had neither.

For months, rumors had been circulating that Ella would sell the place as soon as her mother went to heaven. Three months ago, she'd passed on. Finally, today, Ella had kept her promise and held an auction.

And he had finally gotten out of his older brother's shadow.

Almost against his will, Loyal looked across the yard to a lone bench on the driveway. There sat Ella Hostetler. *Plain Ella*, they'd all called her when they were children.

As if she felt his gaze on her, Ella turned her head. Peered right back at him.

He felt his cheeks flush. "I think I should go speak to Ella."

Calvin grabbed his arm. "Don't."

"I have to, Calvin. She's hurting."

"Of course she is. She just sold off everything she could."

Guilt washed over him. "To me."

"And others." Lowering his voice, Calvin said earnestly, "Ella's disappointment is not your fault. If you didn't spend your hard-earned money on this . . ." He looked around distastefully. "This *place*, someone else would have."

Loyal jerked his arm away. Why did his older brother never cease to be the voice of authority on every single subject? "You're making perfect sense, but I have to try to make things better between Ella and me."

"There is nothing you could say to make things right. At least not today."

"All I'm going to do is tell her I understand . . ."

"You understand what? That you've now given her the money she needed to move on with her life?" Calvin lowered his voice. "Loyal, I do understand your motives, and I even understand Ella's pain. But it's not like she's been a friend of ours. In school, she never played with the rest of us; she always had her head in a book. And since then, she's kept to herself."

Loyal had the sinking suspicion that she would have put a book away if kids had ever invited her to play.

"Let her be," Calvin whispered again. "If anything, your presence will embarrass her. The folks who haven't left yet will watch. And then they'll talk. It's better just to keep your distance."

What his brother said made sense. He turned away and went back to inspecting the stalls.

But every so often, Loyal still felt her gaze on him.

And still felt Ella's pain.

Mary Lou Zinsser

SHELLEY SHEPARD GRAY is the beloved author of the Seasons of Sugarcreek series as well as the Sisters of the Heart series, including *Hidden*, *Wanted*, and *Forgiven*. Before writing, she was a teacher in both Texas and Colorado. She now writes full-time and lives in southern Ohio with her husband and two children. When not writing, Shelley volunteers at church, reads, and enjoys walking her miniature dachshund on her town's scenic bike trail.

Shelley Shepard Gray

BOOKS BY
SHELLEY SHEPARD GRAY

SISTERS OF THE HEART

HIDDEN

To escape a love gone wrong, a young woman runs to the one place she knows she's safe—the Amish heartland. But her chance at happiness may be stolen away by the man from her past.

WANTED

For a split second, Katie feels certain she is about to receive everything she's ever wanted—until a message from her past arrives and threatens to expose her darkest secrets.

FORGIVEN

When tragedy strikes, a brother and sister find themselves facing a situation that will shape the rest of their lives. Sometimes, a simple apology just isn't enough…

GRACE
A Christmas Sisters of the Heart Novel

When two unexpected visitors show up at the town's bed-and-breakfast hoping to stay for Christmas, the Brenneman family must test their commitment to hospitality.

SEASONS OF SUGARCREEK

WINTER'S AWAKENING

As the coldest winter on record blows into Sugarcreek, three young people must struggle to determine the path of their futures.

SPRING'S RENEWAL

Two people must determine how much they'll sacrifice for a chance at true love, as a flash flood threatens to destroy everything they hold dear.

AUTUMN'S PROMISE

Despite being from different worlds, an English woman and an Amish man fall in love and must decide if either one can give up the life they know for the sake of true love.

www.ShelleyShepardGray.com